GHOST DOG
SECRETS

PEG KEHRET

GHOST DOG
SECRETS

SCHOLASTIC INC.
New York Toronto London Auckland
Sydney Mexico City New Delhi Hong Kong

ISBN 978-0-545-38989-1

12 11 10 9 8 7 6 5 4 3 2 1   11 12 13 14 15 16/0

Printed in the U.S.A.   40

First Scholastic printing, September 2011

Designed by Irene Vandervoort

For Eric Konen
Thanks for muscle-man chores, game marathons,
granny/grandson dates, and fun overnight visits.

I first saw the dog chained to a tree on a frigid October morning. Icy rain pelted him, and his tail drooped between his hind legs as he watched the cars pass his yard. He had no shelter.

"Mom!" I said. "Look at that poor dog! He doesn't even have a doghouse."

She glanced at the dog. "Not everyone takes care of their animals, Rusty," she said, and quickly returned her attention to the slick road. Since she was already annoyed with me for missing the school bus, I didn't say anything more, but the image of the dog stayed with me. While my sixth-grade teacher, Mrs. Webster, tried to interest the class in the industrial revolution, I looked at the sleet blowing sideways against the window and thought how cold that dog must be.

My attention returned to the classroom when I heard the word *quiz*. Mrs. Webster's favorite trick was to spring an unannounced quiz on the class. When we complained, she always said, "If I told you that you were going to be tested, most of you would study the night before, but the point of education is that you should study whether you think you'll be tested or not. You need to do your homework every night and keep up with the reading assignments. A surprise quiz lets me know who is doing that, and it's a good wake-up call for those who are not."

For me, a quiz usually equaled an alarm clock, especially if the test was in math.

That day, though, I was lucky. The quiz said, "Write two paragraphs about the book you're reading for free reading." Each student was supposed to read for thirty minutes every evening. Since we could read anything we wanted (as long as it was age appropriate—Gerald Langston had once claimed he spent the entire thirty minutes reading *Goodnight Moon*) it was my favorite homework and the only assignment I did consistently. I quickly jotted down two paragraphs about my current book.

I finished, looked up, and caught Gerald peering at my paper. When he saw me look at him, Gerald turned around and began to write on his own paper. I dropped my pencil on the floor as an excuse to bend closer to see Gerald's paper. Just as I thought, he had written about the same book that I was reading. Ha! Fat chance that Gerald had read anything. Gerald ignored me as he scribbled away.

It's easy to write a report on a book you have not read. All you have to do is talk about the fast-paced plot or the intriguing characters or the author's use of similes. As long as you've put the title in the first sentence, the rest of it sounds true, and I was pretty sure Gerald would get away with his deception.

All the kids knew that Gerald cheated, but he never got caught and nobody wanted to be the one who squealed on him. In Heath School, being a tattletale was more of a disgrace than being a cheater. I retrieved my pencil, then turned my paper over so that Gerald couldn't copy anything more.

While I waited for Mrs. Webster to tell us to pass our papers forward, I made a mental list of the reasons why I don't like Gerald:

1. He cheats.

2. He makes fun of Matthew because Matthew's dad is in prison, saying stuff like, "Seen the jailbird lately?" It seems to me it would be hard enough to have your dad get sent to prison for armed robbery without being reminded of it every day.

3. In fourth grade our teacher had a classroom guinea pig, and Gerald used to poke the guinea pig with the point of his pencil. Shannon Whitehouse finally told the teacher about that and nobody called her a tattletale. I wished I'd been the one to stand up for the guinea pig.

4. Gerald thinks it's funny to trip people. He

sticks his leg into the aisle at the last second as someone walks past. Twice I've stumbled and had to catch myself, and once I landed on my hands and knees. I'm not the only one he trips, but because we are seated alphabetically and Larson (me, Rusty Larson) comes right after Langston, I sit directly behind Gerald and have to pass his desk to get anywhere in the room.

I was working on number five when Mrs. Webster said we could put our papers on her desk on our way to lunch. I followed Gerald and put my paper on top of his. I hoped Mrs. Webster wouldn't think that I had copied from him. I didn't worry too much about that, since I had written about the specific things I had liked in the book. Unless Gerald had actually read the book, which I doubted, his paper would be only generalizations.

During lunch I complained about Gerald to my best friend, Andrew. In first grade, Andrew and I had formed a "club" called the Knights of the Royal Underpants. One of the club activities was to make up alliterative three-word phrases that we called *threesomes*. We didn't hold club meetings anymore, but we still created threesomes and sometimes called each other by our club names. I was Mighty Muscles Man. Andrew was Exalted Exciting Expert.

"Gerald's hopeless," Andrew said. "Ignore him."

The afternoon dragged and I found myself thinking about the dog again.

When we had to write a poem for our language arts unit, I wrote:

CHAINED MISERY

Icy rain pounds brown-black fur
Water drips from pointed ears
As I ride past, dog's image blurs
Through wet window, and my tears.

Fur is singular and blurs is plural, so they don't really rhyme, but time was up before I could fix that. Although Mrs. Webster says a first draft is not a finished poem, we are never given enough time to revise anything.

We ended the class day with a discussion about litter. One of Mrs. Webster's goals in life is to turn all of her students into involved citizens who help solve the problems of the world. At the beginning of the year, we had a guest speaker from Habitat for Humanity who talked about building houses for people who can't afford them, and last week we had a speaker from the Department of Ecology who told us what kind of evidence to look for if we think someone has a meth-amphetamine lab on their property. He said even if we don't think there's a meth lab in our neighborhood, we should all be knowledgeable about how to tell. Our next guest speaker was going to talk about recycling.

Kids sometimes mention a community problem in class, hoping Mrs. Webster will get distracted and talk about it instead of having us do our work.

That day, Hayley said, "The playground area at Kennedy Park is a mess. Somebody ought to do something about it."

"You are somebody," Mrs. Webster said. "Each of us is somebody."

We all looked at her.

"When we say, 'Somebody ought to do something,'" she continued, "we're wishing someone else would solve a problem, but perhaps we are the ones who should take action."

"My parents would never let me go to the park and pick up the trash," Hayley said. "Some of it is really nasty stuff, like pee in bottles."

"Ewww," said Jordan. "Gross!"

"What else could you do to solve the problem, besides cleaning up the park yourself?" Mrs. Webster asked.

Ideas flew. "Call the parks department and complain." "Write a letter to the editor of the local paper." "Ask a service organization, maybe the Boy Scouts, to have a cleanup day." "Go do it ourselves but wear disposable gloves and take those gripper things that let you pick stuff up without touching it."

"All excellent suggestions," said Mrs. Webster. "Remember that *you* are the someone in the phrase 'Someone ought to do something about that.' Each of you. Me too. We are all the someone who needs to take action." She walked to the board where today's homework assignment was written. When she erased it, a few kids cheered; the rest of us waited to see what would happen next.

"I've changed your homework assignment," she said. "Instead of math, I want each of you to think of a problem that you personally can help to solve."

I made up my mind right then that I was going to help that dog. As soon as I got home from school, I'd ride my bike back to where I'd seen him. I didn't know what I planned to do when I got there. If the dog was gone, I wouldn't have to do anything except think of a different problem for my homework. But if he was still tied to the tree, I knew I was the someone who had to help him. I just hadn't figured out yet how I would do it.

The dismissal bell finally rang, and I bolted out the door. The school bus took a less direct route from school to my house than the one Mom had driven that morning, so it didn't pass the yard where I'd seen the dog. I couldn't quit thinking about him, though. After I ate some toast with peanut butter and drank a glass of apple juice, I rode my bike to where the dog had been. He was still there, chained to the same tree, asleep on the cold muddy ground.

He looked up when I stopped my bike.

"Hi, dog," I said. "I'm your friend, Rusty."

He stood, looking wary. He was a German shepherd, with a long, bushy tail. He was full grown but he looked young. A year old, maybe. Or two? Since I had never had a pet myself, my knowledge of dogs was limited to the dogs my friends had and to what I'd read or seen on TV.

A row of ribs pushed against his fur on each side. I looked around the yard and saw no bowls for food or water. I should have brought food for him. An owner mean enough to leave the dog chained to a tree all day in the rain probably didn't feed him properly.

As I looked at him, something brushed against my leg. I glanced down but saw nothing. I looked behind me. Nothing there, either.

"I'll be back," I told him, and I pedaled away. There was a convenience store two blocks down the street. I bought a hot dog and took it back to the dog.

I got off my bike and walked slowly toward the dog. He backed away as I approached him. He didn't growl or act threatening, but he clearly did not want me to come closer. When I was near enough to be within reach of his chain, I broke the hot dog into quarters. Using the wrapping paper as a plate, I laid the pieces of hot dog and bun on the ground where he could reach them. Then I returned to my bicycle.

The dog kept a watchful eye on me as he gobbled the food. When he had finished, which took about one second, I went toward him, and again he backed away.

"Good dog," I said. "You're a fine dog." He didn't wag his tail or respond in any way. I knew I needed to earn his trust before I tried to pet him.

"I'll come to see you again tomorrow," I told him. "I'll bring more food." Then I picked up the hot-dog wrapper and rode back home.

CHAPTER TWO

The next day, Mrs. Webster asked, "Did you think of a problem that you personally might be able to help solve?"

Several hands shot up.

"I'm going to ask my youth group at church to collect canned goods for the food bank," said Kylie.

Tyler said, "My neighbor is old and uses a cane. I'm going to rake the leaves in her yard."

Lexi said, "My mom said I can go with her when she volunteers at the library. I'm going to help shelve the returned books."

Mrs. Webster beamed at all of us. "Gerald?" she said. "Did you think of a problem you could help solve?"

Gerald said, "I was thinking I could murder my stupid sister."

Mrs. Webster's smile disappeared. "That might solve one problem," she said, "but what bigger problems would it create?"

Gerald shrugged.

Marci said, "I saw a news report last night about a puppy mill that got raided. It was horrible! The sheriff's deputies took more than a hundred dogs out of one house, and they were all filthy and covered with fleas and some were sick. I'd like to help them, but I don't know how."

"What's a puppy mill?" asked Tyler.

Mrs. Webster said, "A puppy mill is a business run by unscrupulous people whose dogs are bred to have litter after litter, as fast as they can, and who then sell the puppies, usually to pet stores. The dog parents are treated as machinery in a factory, not as living beings. Many spend their whole lives in cages."

"I saw that report, too," said Lexi. "Three of the dogs had a stump in place of one of their legs."

"Often the dogs are inbred," Mrs. Webster said, "which causes birth defects."

"Many of them were sick," Marci said, "but they had received no veterinary care."

"Puppy mills are a disgrace," Mrs. Webster said, "and I hope the people who ran this one get prosecuted for animal cruelty."

I had never seen Mrs. Webster so angry. Usually she was calm and tried to make sure we thought about all sides of an issue, but this time it was clear that the puppy mill infuriated her.

Everyone began talking at once. The class was outraged about the puppy mill and quickly agreed that we wanted to help these dogs. "We can make it a class project," Marci said.

"We can raise money for them or help to find them good homes."

"I'll take one," said Gerald. "I could train it to keep my sister out of my room."

I hoped whoever was responsible for the puppies would be careful about who got to adopt them.

"They may not be available for adoption right away," Mrs. Webster said. "Sometimes in cases like this, the animals are considered evidence in the cruelty case, and they can't be adopted until the trial is held."

This statement brought more outrage from the students.

The room buzzed with suggestions. We had many ideas about how we could help but we all agreed on one thing: we wanted to do *something* to help those puppy mill dogs.

"I'll contact the shelter where they were taken," Mrs. Webster said, "and find out what they need."

When we came back after lunch she said, "I've spoken to the Humane Society, where the puppies are being housed. They need blankets, dog food, laundry detergent, towels, and money. Five of the dogs are in need of urgent veterinary care, including two that need surgery. One dog's teeth are so rotten that he cannot keep his tongue in his mouth. He needs dental care immediately. The people who run the shelter are determined to help these dogs, but they are mostly volunteers and they don't yet have funds to pay for all of it."

"Let's have a bake sale," said Hayley.

"And a car wash," said Andrew.

"If we do a car wash, maybe we could do a dog wash, too," Emily said.

"We could collect old towels and blankets," I said.

Mrs. Webster wrote all of the ideas on the board. When the list had grown to fifteen, she had each of us write down the three that we would most like to do. While we were at recess, she tallied the results.

"Collecting dog food, towels, and blankets was your first choice," she said. "Second choice is a bake sale, and third is to do something creative, such as make bookmarks about animals, and sell them."

She divided us into three groups. Each was supposed to make the plans for how to carry out our assigned idea. I was in the group that would collect blankets, towels, and dog food. Andrew was in that group, too.

For most class projects, Mrs. Webster split up friends, putting pals in different groups, but this time she let us be together. I think she wanted as much enthusiasm and coop-eration as possible for this project because she wanted us to succeed in helping the dogs. She volunteers for an animal rescue group and sometimes showed us photos of her own rescued dogs, Shakespeare and Hemingway.

I lingered after class until everyone else had left. Then I asked Mrs. Webster, "How did the sheriff know about the puppy mill?"

"A concerned citizen made a complaint," she said.

"So if you know about a dog that's not being cared for, you should call the sheriff?"

"It's difficult to prove a case of animal cruelty," Mrs. Webster said. "It helps if you have documentation such as photos or video, or witnesses who will testify, but certainly you should always try to help the animal. If you personally know of a dog that's being mistreated, you should tell your mom or some other trusted adult. They can help you decide if you need to call the authorities."

"Okay," I said, but I was not ready to tell Mom or anyone else about the dog.

"Is it the dog in your poem?" Mrs. Webster asked.

I nodded.

"It's a wonderful poem, Rusty," she said. She didn't ask anything else about the dog who had inspired it, but as I walked toward the door she added, "You are always welcome to talk to me about a problem."

"Thanks," I said, but I kept going.

• • •

When I got home, I took two of Mom's old aluminum pie tins and a bottle of water. I cut up some leftover pot roast and cooked carrots and put the food in a plastic bag. As I worked I thought about the puppy mill puppies and about the chained dog, innocent animals who were suffering because of uncaring humans.

When we worked on our writing in language arts, Mrs. Webster always said it's better to be specific than general. That advice seemed to apply to my current situation, not just to my writing. The puppy mill dogs were a general problem; the dog that was chained to the tree was specific. All the dogs led unhappy, uncomfortable lives. They all needed help. I'd work with my group to collect supplies for the dogs at the shelter, but probably lots of other people would come forward to help those dogs, since their sad plight had been broadcast on TV.

Nobody else was helping the dog that was chained out in the rain. Only me. I would help that one specific dog.

I got my camera and put it in my backpack with the food, water, and pie tins. Mrs. Webster had said photos would prove that the animal was being mistreated, so I planned to take a picture every day, showing the dog chained up with no food, no water, and no place to get out of the rain.

My camera has a feature that will put the date at the bottom of the photo. One picture might not prove anything, but if I had proof that this happened day after day, it ought to carry some weight. When I got to the dog's yard, I found him in the same place he'd been the day before. Had he been there all night? Probably. People who would leave a dog chained up with no food and no shelter would not be likely to take the dog inside at night. I wondered if he'd had anything to eat since the hot dog I had given him.

I got the camera out of my backpack and held it up, staying back far enough to clearly show the barren surroundings and the chain. I didn't want a close-up shot because I wanted it to be clear that he had no shelter.

If I had a dog, I'd let him sleep on my bed with me, and I'd brush him and play with him every day. I can't have a dog, or any pet, because Mom says we can't afford it and nobody's home all day to take care of it.

Things might have been different if my dad were still here. I know he liked dogs because I've seen old pictures of him when he was a teenager, hugging his mutt, Banjo. Dad was killed by a roadside bomb in Iraq when I was eight years old. I keep a picture of him in his army uniform next to my bed. I miss him a lot.

I know Mom misses him, too. Losing him has made her cautious about everything we do, especially if it costs money or involves taking on any extra responsibility. I'm not a bad boy, but I guess I'm all she can handle.

As I pushed the button on the camera, I felt a gentle nudge on the back of my leg. It felt exactly as if a dog had poked me softly with his snout, but when I looked there was no dog. No animal of any kind. A faint shiver ran along the back of my neck. It hadn't bothered me yesterday when I felt something brush my leg. I assumed it had been an odd gust of wind or a twitchy muscle. But this time, it was definitely not the wind. Something—someone?—had poked me. I felt cold, as if the temperature had suddenly dropped about twenty degrees.

I put the camera away and gave the dog his food and water. The dog acted the same as he had the first day; he backed away from me and watched me warily. I put the meat and carrots in one pie tin and poured water in the other, then left them both where the dog could reach them. He slinked toward the food, making sure I stayed out of range. When he finished eating, he drank some of the water.

Instead of watching him eat, I kept glancing around, checking for any movement. The yard was empty. Whatever had poked me was not there.

When the dog finished eating and drinking, I went forward to pick up the pie tins. I wanted to leave the water for him, but I didn't want the dog's owner to know that I was helping the dog, so I had to take both pie tins home with me.

"Good dog," I said. "I'll bring food to you every day." He

backed away so I couldn't reach him, just like before. I had to watch where I stepped, as nobody bothered to scoop in this yard. Some of the dog piles had been there so long they had fuzzy gray mold on top.

The house on the property was set far back from the street and surrounded by a high, thick hedge. The driveway that led to the house curved as it passed the hedge, so the house didn't show from the street. I could glimpse only one corner of a small structure with peeling brown paint. At least I didn't have to worry that anyone inside the house would notice me.

Although the house was small, the dirt yard was large— much bigger than my front yard. Except for the shrubs around the house and the tree to which the dog was chained, there were no plants. The houses in this area all had big lots but none were landscaped or cared for. The house across the street had what looked like a sheet tacked up over the window to keep people from seeing inside. An old clothes washer rusted in that front yard. It seemed as if the people who lived on this street had decided that home and yard maintenance were all too much trouble, and they weren't going to bother anymore.

The good result of this lack of interest was that there were no neighbors out in their yards, watching me.

I mounted my bike. I turned for one last look at the dog

before I rode away—and nearly crashed the bike. I braked, put my feet on the sidewalk, and stared. The dog stood where he always did, in the middle of the dirt yard, but beside him, staring back at me, was another dog. Not a real dog—a see-through dog, a dog made of cloud wisps, an all-white dog that seemed to float just above the ground.

A dog's ghost. It had to be. I shivered. Did I believe in ghosts? I had never given it any thought, one way or the other. I liked to read ghost stories, but I knew they were fiction— fanciful tales that authors made up. Still, I could think of no other explanation for what I was seeing. Is this what had brushed against my leg yesterday and nudged me today? Was the ghost trying to tell me something?

I laid my bike down and walked slowly toward the two dogs. Both dogs stood still, watching me approach. The ghost was—had been?—a female collie, with shaggy fur, a long snout, and pointy ears. When I was about five feet away, the real dog backed up. The instant he moved, the ghost dog disappeared. She simply vanished! One second she was hovering in the air beside the real dog, and the next second she was gone. There was no *poof* sound. No dramatic flash of light. She was there, and then she wasn't.

I waited a few minutes to see if the ghost dog would reappear. When she didn't, I got on my bike and rode home, puzzling over what I had witnessed.

• • •

I washed the pie tins and put them in my bedroom, ready for tomorrow. Then I turned on the computer and Googled "ghost dog" to see what would come up. Most of the entries referred to a samurai action film.

I sat on my bed and debated what to do next. After a few minutes I went downstairs, opened the telephone directory, and found a nonemergency number for the sheriff's department.

"I want to report a dog that isn't being cared for," I said.

"One moment, please. I'll connect you with our animal control officer."

A few seconds later, a voice said, "This is Heidi Kellogg."

"I want to report a dog that's being neglected," I said.

"Do you have proof of neglect?"

"He's chained to a tree all the time, with no food or water."

"How long has the dog been there?"

"I don't know. I noticed him yesterday, and he's still there today."

"Before I can do anything, I need proof of ongoing neglect or of actual abuse," Heidi said.

"I took a picture of him today."

"That's a start. The best proof would be to have surveillance video showing that the dog is not given food or water for thirty-six hours," she said.

"I don't have a video camera. I was going to take a picture every day."

"Do that," she said. "In a week, if you still think the dog needs help, call me back."

"A week! We can't wait that long to help him. He needs help now!"

"Have you been there at night? Are you sure the owner doesn't feed and water the dog then?"

"I haven't been there at night," I admitted, "but there's no bowl of water or empty dish and the dog's really skinny."

"I tell you what. Give me the address where the dog is, and I'll look to see if there have been other complaints about animal abuse there."

"I don't know the exact address," I said, "but I can tell you where the house is."

"I need the house number and street."

Of course she did. What was I thinking?

"Keep an eye on the dog for a week and if you still think it's being mistreated, take pictures for proof, if you can, and then call back with the specific address."

I hung up feeling stupid. What a moron move that was, not writing down the address before I called the sheriff. How had I thought they were going to find the dog without an address?

I sat by the phone for a minute composing threesomes to describe my error:

Major mammoth mistake.

Big basic blunder.

Next I began to describe myself:

Stupid sappy scatterbrain.

Clueless colossal clod.

Finally I decided that berating myself for an honest mistake didn't help solve the problem. The only way to help the dog was to document his situation and then report it.

I put a piece of paper and a pencil in my backpack, to be sure I had them tomorrow. I would get the address, and I would write down the date and time of each of my visits, along with the weather. I'd create a journal of times when I'd found the dog alone with no food or shelter. When I had enough dates and photos and comments, it would be proof of neglect.

Meanwhile, I had promised the dog I'd bring him food every day, so I needed to figure out how to do that. I couldn't take leftovers all the time because Mom would notice and ask questions. I couldn't afford to buy a hot dog for him every day, either.

I counted the money that I had left from my birthday— more than ten dollars— then walked to the grocery store to buy a bag of dog food. I read the labels and tried to choose one that was nutritious and not full of ingredients I'd never heard of before. What is chicken by-product meal? I didn't want to feed my dog junk that I wouldn't want to eat myself.

My dog. A prickle of excitement made my scalp tingle.

I knew he wasn't really my dog, of course, but he was starting to seem as if he belonged to me. Even though he was still afraid of me, I believed he would learn to trust me and then to love me. I loved him already.

Back at home, I took a small plastic bag from the kitchen drawer and filled it with dog food. I could carry the bag in my backpack, along with the pie tins and the water. I hid the large sack of dog food in my closet, draping an old pair of jeans over it. I knew Mom would not approve of my feeding the dog. I figured if she didn't know about it, she couldn't tell me not to do it and, therefore, I was not disobeying any rules.

That night, I woke suddenly. I lay still, listening, wondering what had awakened me. The numbers on the digital clock beside my bed said 12:16.

Just past midnight.

It felt cold in my room. Even under the blankets, I was chilly. I wondered if Mom had opened a window and forgotten to close it. When she changes the sheets on my bed, she usually opens a window, even in winter, to "air out the room."

Intending to walk across the room to check the window, I groggily swung my feet over the side of the bed. It was like sticking my legs into a tank of ice water.

Instantly wide awake, I looked beside my bed. The dog ghost stared back at me. The cold air that swirled around my feet came from her.

The dog ghost did not appear menacing. She didn't bare her teeth or act as if she wanted to bite me. Instead, she trotted to my bedroom door, which was closed. She turned back, as if to say, *Let's go.*

CHAPTER THREE

I put on a pair of sneakers and my bathrobe, opened the bedroom door, and followed the ghost down the stairs. She went straight to the front door, then stood there watching me.

"I can't go out with you," I whispered. "It's past midnight. I'm supposed to be in bed."

The dog waited.

I unlocked the door and opened it. The ghost dog trotted outside and partway down the sidewalk. Then she looked back, waiting for me.

Curiosity welled up inside me. What did the collie want to show me? I followed the dog's ghost for half a block. *I shouldn't do this,* I thought. *For one thing, it's dangerous to go wandering about alone in the middle of the night. Also, Mom would ground me for a month if she found out and then how would I take food to my real dog?*

My concern about getting caught and not being able to feed the chained dog won out over my curiosity about what the collie's ghost wanted me to see. I went back home.

I had relocked the front door and started up the stairs when Mom appeared in the hallway above me. "Is anything wrong?" she asked.

"I was hungry," I said.

"I woke up and didn't know why," Mom said. "I must have heard you in the kitchen."

"Sorry," I said as I climbed the stairs. "I tried to be quiet."

"Next time turn on a light," Mom said. "You could trip on something, walking around in the dark."

After checking my bedroom window, which was closed, I went back to bed, but it took me a long time to fall asleep. I kept expecting the collie's ghost to reappear. Eventually I fell into a restless sleep, jerking awake when my alarm went off.

At school, Mrs. Webster let us work on our puppy mill projects all morning. My group decorated three large round bins that she had brought in. We would use them to collect blankets, towels, and dog food. After much discussion, we decided to put one bin inside the main entrance to the school and one bin outside the doors to the gym, where parents came to watch basketball games, gymnastics meets, and other student events.

"Let's put the third bin at Safeway," Marci suggested. "Everybody buys groceries, so lots of people would see it, and they could buy dog food right there."

We agreed that this was a good plan. Mrs. Webster said we needed to write a letter to the store manager, requesting permission and explaining where the collected food would go.

"Why can't we just ask him?" I wondered. "If he says yes, we can put the bin in the store right then."

"You will ask in person," she said, "but he'll need the request in writing. You should have it with you."

There were six people on my committee. Mrs. Webster said only two of us should visit the grocery store manager, so we had to choose who would do it.

"Whoever goes should do it right away," I said. "Like today."

Everyone agreed that the sooner the bin was placed in the store, the better.

"I can't go today," Marci said. "I'm going to visit my grandma after school."

Andrew looked at me. "Do you want to go?" he asked. "I'm available."

I hesitated. If I went with Andrew to talk to the Safeway manager and place the bin in his store, it wouldn't leave much time to feed my dog before Mom got home.

Before I responded, Lexi spoke up. "I'll go," she said. "My mom picks me up every day, and we go right past Safeway on our way home. Half the time she stops there anyway."

"I can go with you," Hayley offered, "if your mom wouldn't mind taking me home after we talk to the manager."

We spent the next forty-five minutes composing the letter for Lexi and Hayley to take with them.

Twice a week our class goes to the library for half an hour, right before lunch. That day I looked up ghosts in the library catalog and then went to the section that has books about ghosts. None of them were specifically about animal ghosts but I figured I'd browse through them, in case there was some mention of a ghost dog.

I got so absorbed in my reading that I didn't notice when the rest of my class left the library. A tap on my shoulder startled me. "It's lunchtime, Rusty," Mrs. Webster said.

I closed the book I had been skimming and stood up. "You can check those out, if you want to," Mrs. Webster said.

"I'm done with them," I said. "They aren't quite what I was looking for."

I put the books back on the shelf and hurried to the cafeteria.

"Greetings and salutations, Mighty Muscles Man," Andrew said as I plunked my tray down on the table across from him.

"Hey, Exalted Exciting Expert," I replied. Two girls at the end of the table looked at each other and rolled their eyes.

"No eavesdropping, ladies," I said. They moved to the next table.

"You're late," Andrew said. "I thought maybe you'd gone on a strict diet and were skipping lunch."

"No way," I said. "I'm starving." I took a big bite of pizza and drizzled dressing on my salad.

"How come you didn't want to take the collection bin to Safeway?" he asked.

"I didn't say I didn't want to."

"You weren't exactly eager to volunteer."

"Lexi and Hayley will do a good job of asking the manager," I said.

"True. Probably better than we would have done. I always get distracted by the candy bar racks that are next to the checkouts. I see them and turn into a greedy guilty glutton." He licked the frosting off a chocolate cupcake. "Do you want to shoot some hoops after school?"

"I can't. I've got stuff to do."

"What kind of stuff?"

I hesitated, then said, "It's a secret."

Andrew's eyebrows went up. He gave me his famous laser look, which always makes me feel as if he's reading my mind. Then he leaned toward me and whispered, "Is there a girl involved?"

"No!"

"Just asking. First you don't volunteer to take the puppy mill bin to Safeway, and now it turns out it's because you have some secret activity." There was a brief, awkward silence. I knew he was hoping I'd explain.

I took another bite of pizza.

Andrew said, "How about tomorrow afternoon then?"

I shook my head. "I'm probably going to be busy every day," I said.

"And you can't tell me what you're doing."

"If Mom finds out, I'm grounded for life."

"Hey!" Andrew said. He pointed one finger at his chest. "It's me, remember? Your buddy who swore on the grave of that dead blue jay to always be loyal! The only other member of the Knights of the Royal Underpants and proud creator of threesomes. I'm not telling your mom anything you don't want her to know."

His smile faded, replaced by a frown. "You aren't involved in something illegal, are you? Like shoplifting or stealing hubcaps?"

I pointed at myself and mimicked him: "It's me, remember? Your honest neighborhood Boy Scout and cofounder of the Knights of the Royal Underpants."

"Well, if it's legal, why can't you tell me? Maybe I can do it with you."

The minute he said that, I knew I should tell him about the dog. For one thing, Andrew is smart, and he's good at figuring out solutions to problems. For another, he gets way more allowance than I get and could easily help pay for dog food. Then there was the ghost. Even though the collie's ghost had never acted threatening, it gave me the willies to know she could come into my bedroom while I was sleeping any time she wanted to.

I felt an overwhelming desire to tell someone what was happening, and Andrew was the logical person because I knew I could trust him to keep my secret. Even though we still made up threesomes, we rarely mentioned the club we'd started as six-year-olds. When Andrew brought up the Knights of the Royal Underpants, I knew it was because he really wanted to be in on whatever I was doing every day after school.

"Okay," I said. "Meet me at my house after school."

I ride the school bus home, but Andrew's mom often drives him, so he gets home faster than I do. He rolled up on his bike before I had even peeled my banana.

"I'm all eager, expectant ears," he said.

"You have to swear you won't tell anybody."

"I won't tell unless what you're doing puts you in danger."

I thought about that. What would happen if the dog's owner came home and saw me feeding the dog? He or she might get angry and tell me to leave, but I didn't think I'd be in any danger. They might even thank me.

"I saw a TV news report last night," Andrew said. "Two kids were standing on a freeway overpass, dropping rocks on cars."

I gave him a disgusted look. "That was not me," I said. "That is dangerous, disastrous, and dumb."

"I know. They got caught because the State Patrol helicopter saw them and followed when they tried to run away. I was only giving an example of what I would not keep secret."

I checked my backpack for kibble, dishes, and water, then I put it on. "Let's go," I said.

Andrew didn't ask *where*; he simply nodded and followed me outside.

While we walked to the yard where the dog was chained, I told Andrew about the dog and that I was feeding him. When we were almost there, I said, "There is one more thing I need to tell you."

"Okay."

"Besides the dog I'm helping, there's another dog. Not a real dog. I think it's a dog's ghost."

"Have you seen it?" he asked.

"Twice. And I've felt her two other times, nudging my leg with her nose."

"What does she look like? Can you tell what kind of dog she is?"

"She's a collie but she's all white, even her eyes, and I can see right through her. You know how steam flows off the roof sometimes when the sun comes out after a cold spell, or how you can see your breath in winter? Well, it's as if that steam or breath was formed in the shape of a dog."

"Does she move?"

"She walks like a real dog, except that her feet don't always touch the ground. She sort of floats. She came to my house last night while I was asleep. She stood next to my bed and woke me up."

"Cool."

I wasn't sure what I had expected Andrew to say but, as usual, he surprised me. The idea of a ghost in my bedroom, dog or human, made me uneasy—not scared, exactly, but nervous because I didn't know what to expect. Andrew wasn't at all anxious about possibly encountering a dog's ghost.

"What happened? What did she do after you woke up?"

"She tried to get me to follow her."

Andrew looked impressed. "Did you?"

"I went about half a block and then I turned back. It's a good thing I didn't go any farther because Mom got up and would have caught me if I'd been going down the sidewalk after the collie."

"Man, I hope she's there today," Andrew said. "It would be awesome to see a dog ghost."

When we reached the dog's yard, he was tied in his usual spot. I took a picture of him and told Andrew what Heidi

Kellogg at animal control had said. "I'm keeping a journal, too," I said.

Andrew watched as I offered food and water while the dog stayed as far away from me as he could get.

"How long have you been feeding him?" Andrew asked as we watched the dog eat.

"This is the third day."

"Do you see the ghost now?" Andrew asked.

"No. Do you?"

Andrew shook his head. "Maybe she won't come around when there's more than one of us here." He sounded disappointed but I was relieved. I was worried enough about the dog who was chained to the tree; I didn't need to worry about a dog ghost, too. If the collie kept away because of Andrew that was fine with me.

"Somebody's been mean to that dog," Andrew said.

"How do you know?"

"Most dogs, once you give them food, they warm right up. This is the third time you've brought him food, and he's clearly hungry, but the dog still acts scared to be near you. He doesn't trust you, even after you've fed him every day. I'll bet someone beats him or hurts him somehow."

I swallowed the lump in my throat. I didn't want to think about somebody hitting the dog, or worse.

"We should rescue him," Andrew said.

"What?"

"It doesn't really help him that much to bring food and then leave him chained up like this, especially if the person who chains him is mean to him. It's getting really cold at night now, and we'll have snow soon. Animals need more food when it's cold, and they need shelter. Who knows what happens to him at night when the owner comes home? We need to take him with us. We need to get him out of here."

"How can we take him with us? I can't even get close enough to pet him."

"You will. If you keep bringing food every day and talking soft to him like you're doing, he'll learn that you aren't going to hurt him, and eventually he'll let you get close to him. When he does, we can unhook that chain and snap on a leash and take him away from here."

"That would be stealing."

"Would it? Or would it be rescuing a dog who needs help?"

More than once in our long friendship, Andrew had talked me into doing something that got me in trouble. I picked up the empty pie tins. "As soon as I have a few more photos and journal entries," I said, "I'll call animal control back and give Heidi the exact address. She might take the dog away from his owner."

"And she might not. Somehow I don't think a dog chained

to a tree is high on the priority list of people who deal with murders, bank robberies, and abducted children."

"She's the animal control officer," I said. "It's her job to help animals."

"He won't starve to death as long as you keep feeding him," Andrew said, "but without shelter he could freeze to death this winter."

"I'll get Heidi or the sheriff out here before it turns that cold," I said, but even to myself I didn't sound sure. At this time of year, we often get sudden cold spells, where the temperature drops well below freezing. Last Halloween, Andrew and I had gone trick-or-treating in the snow.

Andrew gave me his laser look. "Someone ought to save that dog," he said.

I knew he was really telling me that *we* were the someone, just as Mrs. Webster had said.

CHAPTER FOUR

We walked home in silence. My mind churned. Feeding the dog was one thing; actually taking him was a lot more serious. I knew what my mom would say about that, if she ever found out, and yet, I believed Andrew was right. Helping the dog was so important that if the only way to do it was to take him without permission, that's what I needed to do.

It's ironic, I thought. Andrew had been worried that I might be doing something illegal and now he's the one to suggest that we take a dog who doesn't belong to us.

When we got to the greenbelt that adjoins my house, I said, "Do you want to go to the fort for awhile?"

Instead of answering, Andrew took off running, beating me to the fort by several seconds. Our fort was hidden in the trees, where it didn't show from the street. We had built it the summer before, scrounging ends of boards, partial sheets of plywood, and other materials from a Dumpster on the site where a construction crew had been building two houses. We used Andrew's dad's tools.

Except for a box of nails and a padlock, to ensure that nobody else entered our hiding place, the fort had cost us nothing.

We removed the padlock's key from under a big rock, unlocked the crude door, went in, and sat on the two blue plastic milk crates that served as chairs.

"We could keep him here," I said. "He could sleep in the fort at night, and we could take turns coming early in the morning before school to feed him and walk him, and we could both come after school."

"Spoken like a true co-king," Andrew said.

"Or a co-nutcase. We could end up in a heap of trouble if we take that dog."

"He needs a name," Andrew said. "If we're going to rescue him, we can't keep calling him the dog."

"How about Max?"

Andrew shook his head. "I read the results of a survey online," he said. "Max is one of the two most common dog names in the United States."

"What's the other one?"

"Buddy." Andrew unwrapped a stick of gum, broke it in two, and offered half to me. "This is a special dog," he said. "He can't have an ordinary name."

I agreed. We both thought for awhile.

"Let's put our initials together and make up a new name for him," I suggested.

"M-E?" Andrew asked. "Or E-M?"

It took me a second to realize he was using the initials

from the Mighty Muscles Man and Exalted Exciting Expert names, from our old club.

"Not *those* initials," I said.

Andrew smiled, obviously pleased that I had figured out his joke.

"Let's name him Ra," I said. "R for Rusty and A for Andrew."

"I like it," Andrew said. "Ra was an Egyptian sun god. He was one of the very first gods ever."

Andrew often surprised me by knowing stuff like that. I'd long ago given up asking him HOW he knew the odd facts that spewed from his mouth. I just accepted that he did. Andrew read a lot and seemed to remember everything he read. Also, while I used my computer time to play games, he browsed on lots of different Web sites and read about tsunamis and sea otters and poisonous plants. He wasn't show-offy with his knowledge and I enjoyed learning what he told me. Once when Mrs. Webster was talking about how the pioneers prized their horses for helping clear the land, Andrew asked if we knew that horses have 205 bones in their bodies. Nobody else I knew had a head full of such interesting facts.

"An Egyptian sun god?" I said. "Is that a good name for a dog?"

"You noticed him in the first place because he was standing in the rain and cold," Andrew said, "so it's fitting to name him for a sun god. When he starts his new life with his new name, he'll always be warm, like the sun. A cozy, comfy canine."

"The collie's ghost is cold," I said. "When she came into my bedroom, I woke up shivering. It felt like an Arctic wind was blowing around my bed."

"Most ghosts are cold," Andrew said. "I wonder why the dog ghost is there."

"Maybe it's Ra's mother."

"I doubt Ra's mother was a collie. Ra is a German shepherd. He might even be a purebred."

"No one would pay a lot of money for a purebred dog and then leave him chained to a tree all the time."

"Maybe the collie's ghost is jealous because you're feeding Ra and she's trying to scare you away. Cold cranky collie."

"She wasn't trying to scare me off when she came to my room. She wanted me to follow her."

"Perhaps she's luring you into danger. Maybe she never got any attention and now she's angry because you visit Ra."

"Oh, great. All I need is a ghost dog that doesn't want me there."

"She might also be a good dog who's lonely and hangs around Ra because she doesn't have any dog ghost friends."

"I tried to find information about dog ghosts online and didn't find anything useful. I looked in the library, too, and skimmed through all the books about ghosts, which is why I was late for lunch."

"Maybe we should rescue the ghost, too," Andrew said. "They can both stay in the fort."

"No way. How do you rescue a ghost?"

"The collie's ghost could sleep in your room at night."

"You're freaking me out," I said. "I hope the collie's ghost doesn't come again. I only want to help Ra."

"Dangerous dead dog," said Andrew, but he smiled as he said it.

I decided to change the subject. "Ra will need a dog bed, and a different collar, and a leash."

"Let's go to Value Village," Andrew suggested. "I've seen pet items there, and the prices are less than the pet store."

We rode our bikes to Value Village. It's a huge store that sells secondhand goods that people have donated. We found a red retractable leash in good condition for one dollar. The collars were all scruffy, though, as if they'd been worn for years and years. Looking at them made me sad. Probably whoever had donated them did it because their dog had died and they couldn't bear to throw the old collar in the trash.

"We could keep the collar he has," Andrew said.

"It's one of those choke chains," I said. "I don't like it, and besides, I want him to have a fresh start, with everything chosen by us."

"So do I," Andrew said. "Let's wait. Maybe we'll find a good collar at a garage sale."

We didn't see any dog beds. "We could buy him a blanket, instead of a bed," I said. "That's what the shelter dogs use."

We went to the section of the store that sold bedding. The blankets were priced from $4 to $8. The one we liked best, of course, cost $8.

"Why don't we keep one of the donated blankets?" Andrew asked. "We can go to school early and pick out a blanket for Ra from what's in the bin."

"People are donating those blankets to help the rescued puppy mill dogs," I said.

"Ra will be a rescued dog, too. What's the difference?"

"When you ask people to donate to a particular cause, you can't use the donations for something else, even if it is similar."

Andrew shrugged. I'm not sure I had convinced him, but he agreed we should buy a soft old blanket for Ra to sleep on. We found a tan-and-brown plaid blanket for six dollars that we both liked and that looked clean.

We also bought two bright yellow ceramic bowls for Ra's food and water.

"Yellow, like the sun," Andrew said.

We carried our purchases to the checkout where the

checker rang them up and added sales tax. Even with Andrew paying half, I was left with a grand total of twelve cents to my name.

We took our purchases back to the fort. We folded the blanket, making it the right size for Ra. We hung the leash on a nail that we had pounded into one wall. Originally we had put a picture of our Little League baseball team there, only the team lost every game and we didn't want to look at the picture anymore.

That evening Andrew went shopping with his grandma. I got an excited phone call saying he had purchased a collar for Ra. He showed it to me the next day. It was blue with golden suns on it.

"Perfect!" I said.

"Best of all," Andrew said, "my grandma paid for it."

"Didn't she wonder why you wanted a dog collar?"

"I told her our class is collecting things for the animal shelter, to help the rescued puppy mill dogs."

I raised my eyebrows.

"What?" Andrew said.

"This collar isn't for the shelter."

"I never said it was. I wouldn't lie to my grandma."

Andrew may be the smartest kid I know but he isn't always totally ethical. Still, it wasn't as if he had shoplifted the collar. I knew Andrew's grandma had a pampered Pomeranian. If she had known the real reason Andrew wanted a dog collar, she would probably have paid for it anyway.

"I did some research," Andrew said, "and I learned something interesting about dog ghosts."

"Such as?"

"Most are friendly, often hanging around the people they loved, but there are a few reports of vicious ghost dogs who appear to be guarding their former homes and who terrorize anyone who approaches."

"So how do you tell the difference? How do I know if the collie's ghost is friendly or evil?"

Andrew shrugged. "The source didn't say. I guess you know it's vicious if it attacks you."

"That does a lot for my peace of mind."

Andrew spoke in an eerie voice. "Ghastly growling ghost."

"Cut it out," I said. "Since it didn't try to attack me when I was sleeping, I'm going to assume it's a good ghost."

The next day, Lexi and Hayley said the Safeway manager was enthusiastic about having the bin in his store.

"He had seen the puppy mill report on TV," Lexi said, "so we didn't even have to explain."

"My mom says we can leave for school a few minutes early every morning," Hayley said, "and pick up whatever is in the bin."

Mrs. Webster had us make three graphs to record how many blankets, how many towels, and how much dog food we collected. She said every morning the whole class would count the contents of the two school bins, add them to the Safeway donations, and pack them in boxes. Then we'd enter the numbers on our graphs and post the graphs in the hallway outside our room. We also kept a running total of monetary donations. Mrs. Webster put those in a locked metal box which she kept in the school office.

Mrs. Webster said the graphs were a way to keep track of our progress and to let the rest of the classes know the results, but I suspected it was a way to work some math practice into our puppy mill project.

Andrew and I fed Ra again after school. Ra stood up as we approached, but instead of backing away, he stayed where he was as we brought him his food. Andrew watched hopefully for the collie's ghost but it didn't show up.

On Friday, Ra came forward to meet us when we brought the food to him. He even wagged his tail! Andrew and I felt like cheering, but we didn't want to startle him. We smiled at each other.

Always before, Ra had watched warily while we put the dishes down, and he had waited until we walked away before he ate. Now he started to eat while we were still standing beside him. I looked at Andrew, who grinned and gave me a thumbs-up. I waited until Ra had finished, then reached down and put my fingertips on his head. "Good dog," I said softly. "Good boy, Ra."

He let me run my hand down his back, stroking his fur. I kept talking to him and petting him. Then he let Andrew pet him. We rubbed behind his ears and stroked his back.

"Soon," Andrew said.

"Soon," I agreed.

CHAPTER FIVE

Andrew's little sister, Wendy the Whiner, went bowling with us on Saturday. She's six, too young to bowl at the alley where we go, but she likes to hang around and watch. If Wendy had her way, she would go everywhere with Andrew and me. Most of the time we said no, but letting her tag along to the bowling alley was relatively painless. For one thing, if we took Wendy, Andrew's mom would drive us and pick us up. Otherwise we rode our bikes. It was only a couple of miles but after bowling for two hours, neither of us felt much like hopping on a bike.

Andrew asked if he could stay at my house awhile afterward.

"I want to stay, too," Wendy said.

Andrew's mother told Wendy no. She always seemed grateful when we took Wendy with us, and I think she didn't want to push her luck. As soon as she dropped us off, we got ready to go feed Ra.

We were cautious as we approached Ra's yard, watching carefully for any sign that someone might be home. Until now, no one had been there, but we had always gone during the week. Today we heard loud music coming from behind the hedge.

"Uh-oh," I said. "Somebody's in the house."

"Do you think we should leave?" Andrew asked.

I hesitated, looking at the thick shrubs around the house. "Maybe we should come back later," I said, "after dark."

"I'm not sure I can sneak out after dark."

"Me neither."

"I don't really *want* to come here after dark," Andrew admitted.

We stood on the sidewalk at the edge of the property. Ra had seen us and had stood up. I wanted to feed him but I also wanted to get out of there as fast as I could. I had no desire to meet Ra's owner. If he was mean to his dog he was probably mean to kids, too, especially kids who were trespassing on his property and feeding his dog without permission.

A cloud of cold air billowed around my ankles. When I looked down, I saw the ghost dog standing in the dirt beside us.

"She's here," I said.

"Who's here?"

"The collie's ghost."

Andrew's head swiveled. "Where?"

I pointed. "There!"

"I don't see her."

"Do you feel the cold wind?"

Andrew moved closer to me. "I don't feel anything."

He gave me his laser look. "Are you making this up?" he asked.

"No! The ghost dog is right in front of us."

"What's she doing?"

"She's floating slowly toward Ra, but she keeps looking back at us."

Ra watched us, waiting for his meal.

"Ra is hungry," I said. "I think the collie wants us to feed him."

"If you want to give Ra his food," Andrew said, "I'll stand at the end of the driveway and watch the house. If anyone comes, I'll yell and we can both run."

I poured kibble into a pan and walked quickly to Ra. He wagged his tail as I approached. The collie's ghost stood beside him; her tail wagged, too.

While Ra ate the kibble, I poured some water in the second pan and put it down. I realized I no longer felt the cold air. I looked around.

The collie had disappeared.

As soon as Ra finished eating and drinking, Andrew and I hurried away, relieved that nobody had seen us.

That night the collie's ghost appeared in my bedroom again. I had just gone to bed and was half-asleep, half-awake when the cold air blew across my face. I opened my eyes. The ghost was standing on her hind legs, with her front paws on the bed beside me. Even in the dark, her white fur was clearly visible. As soon as I looked at her, she pawed at the blanket. I didn't hear the scratch of her toenails, but the blanket moved.

This time, I wasn't afraid. I wasn't sure why the ghost had come, but she didn't seem to want to hurt me or even to frighten me. "What do you want?" I whispered. She pawed at the blanket again. I wondered if she could hear me. I wondered if she could bark.

"You want me to get up, don't you?" I said. The dog left the side of my bed and glided to the door.

"I can't go outside with you," I told her. The dog lifted one front foot and scratched at the door.

I put a pair of jeans on over my pajamas, slipped my feet into my flip-flops, and grabbed my jacket. Then I picked up my camera, aimed it at the dog ghost, and snapped. The flash briefly illuminated the room but did not startle the collie. I opened my bedroom door and looked toward Mom's bedroom. Her door was closed. No light showed under the crack. I put the camera in my jacket pocket.

The collie's ghost was already partway down the stairs. I followed quietly. *I hope I don't regret this,* I thought.

I unlocked the front door, stepped outside, and closed the door softly behind me. When I got to the sidewalk, I looked up at Mom's bedroom window. It was still dark. I turned and walked quickly down the street.

I followed the ghost, but I already knew where she was taking me. I felt like Timmy in one of those old Lassie movie reruns that Mom and I used to watch. I remember snickering at those films and thinking, no dog is that smart. Now I wasn't so sure.

When we reached Ra's yard, he wasn't there. One end of the chain still circled the tree, but the other end lay in the dirt. Ra was gone. Had he broken loose? Was he running through the streets? Is that what the collie's ghost wanted me to know?

Two cars were parked in the driveway near the hedge. Loud rap music throbbed inside the house and harsh voices rose angrily. I couldn't make out what the people said, but I could tell a huge argument was taking place.

The collie trotted up the driveway toward the house, then stopped to look at me. She clearly wanted me to follow, knock on the door, and see what was going on inside, but I knew I couldn't do that. Whoever was in that house would not be pleased to find a twelve-year-old kid on the doorstep, asking about a missing dog.

I got out my camera and snapped a picture of the chain lying on the ground by the tree. I'm not sure why, but I also took a picture of the two cars. Then I turned and ran for home.

Instantly I was running into a strong, icy wind. It was as

if a cold front had suddenly moved down from Canada and the full force of the storm was blowing at my face, trying to keep me from going forward. I put my head down, pushing ahead, but I barely moved. When I looked up, I saw the collie a few yards ahead of me. She faced me head on with her legs braced stiffly, as if she were using all her energy to create a barrier that I couldn't get past.

I stopped running. "I'm sorry," I told her. "I know you want me to go back there, but I can't do it. I want to help Ra, but I can't talk to the people in that house. I need to help Ra my own way. If he's lost, I'll do everything I can to find him. If he's in that house, I . . ." I what? My voice trailed off. "I'm sorry," I said again.

I was glad there wasn't anyone else around. If someone saw me standing there in the middle of the night apologizing to a dog's ghost, they would probably haul me off for a mental evaluation.

I didn't know if the collie could understand me. I didn't even know for sure if she could hear me. All I knew was that the cold wind stopped and I was able to make it home with no more trouble. Mom's window was still dark. I eased inside, locked the door, and tiptoed upstairs to bed.

I didn't sleep, though. I lay there wondering where Ra was. It had been awful to know that he was always chained outside, lying in the dirt no matter what the weather was, but it was worse not to know where he was or what was happening to him. I was certain the collie had tried to alert me to a problem. There was no other explanation. But I didn't know what the difficulty was or what to do about it.

If Ra had somehow escaped, it might be a good thing. Maybe he would be picked up and turned in to the Humane Society and I could talk Mom into letting me adopt him. That way he'd be my dog legally. Still, I didn't like the idea of Ra being loose. He could get hit by a car or get lost or have lots of other bad things happen to him.

There was still the possibility that he had not broken free of his chain but was in the house with those angry people. I remembered Andrew saying, "Someone's been mean to that dog," and I felt as if I might throw up.

I called Andrew the next morning. "Ra's missing," I said, and told him what had happened. "We need to get over there as soon as we can. If he isn't there, we can report him as a lost dog, and we can go to the shelter and look to see if anyone has brought him there."

"I can't do it today," Andrew said. "It's my grandpa's birthday, and I'm spending the day at my grandparents' house. I was going to call you and tell you I can't come this afternoon."

"I'll go by myself," I said.

"Let me know if you find him," Andrew said. "I wish I

could go with you but my parents made it clear that the whole family is going today for Grandpa's birthday. My presence is requested, required, and rewarded."

"Rewarded? What's your reward for going?"

"I'm allowed to continue living with my parents. Actually, I want to go to Grandpa's birthday party, although I wish I could go with you, too. Maybe Ra will be there. Maybe his owner took him inside last night."

I wasn't sure which would be worse—having Ra lost or having him inside with the angry voices.

I couldn't wait until late afternoon when I usually fed Ra. I went as soon as I finished talking to Andrew. I told Mom I was going out for a bike ride, and then I pedaled straight to Ra's house.

I spotted him from a block away, lying in the dirt in his usual place. I had not been aware that I was holding my breath as I turned onto Ra's street, but when I saw him my breath blew out in relief. The collie's ghost lay beside him. It was the first time I'd seen the dog ghost lying down. I wondered if the ghost made Ra feel cold.

Ra did not get up when I got off my bike, even though he saw me.

The house was quiet. The two cars that had been parked in the driveway the night before were gone. I hoped it was early enough that Ra's owner might still be sleeping.

When I went toward Ra, the collie's ghost stood and moved away, but Ra stayed where he was. I knelt beside him. He kept his snout on his front paws. I took a dog biscuit out of my pocket and offered it to him. He didn't take it. Whatever had happened to Ra the night before, it had left him lethargic and uninterested even in food.

I gently slid my hands down his sides. When my fingers touched his haunch, he whimpered. My hand jerked away. "I'm sorry," I whispered. "I didn't mean to hurt you."

But someone else *had* hurt him. I knew that, deep in my bones, even though I didn't have what the sheriff's department would consider proof. Last night, something bad had happened to Ra.

I knew I couldn't wait any longer. I needed to rescue Ra before he got hurt again.

"Tomorrow," I told him. "I have to wait until Andrew's here to help me, but tomorrow we'll take you away from here. I promise."

Ra did not respond. Much as I wanted to stay with him, I couldn't take a chance of being seen. I left him lying in the dirt and climbed on my bike. The collie's ghost lay back down next to Ra.

As soon as I got home, I sent Andrew an urgent e-mail: *Must rescue Ra tomorrow.* Sometimes he checked e-mail from his grandpa's computer. I wished I could text him because he'd get a text message instantly, but Mom refused to pay the extra monthly fee for text messaging.

I spent most of the day fretting. What if Ra still couldn't stand up when Andrew and I were ready to take him? He was too big for us to carry him. He probably needed to be seen by a veterinarian. How would we manage that without telling anyone that we had a dog?

I called the sheriff's department again and asked for Heidi Kellogg. I got her voice mail, which said she'd be back in the office on Monday. I didn't want to leave a message, so I dialed again and talked to the person who answered.

"I want to report a dog that's been mistreated," I said. Then, before I was asked, I gave the address. "I have pictures, one taken every afternoon last week, that show he was kept chained up with no food or water," I said. "Today he acts as if he's hurt, like maybe somebody hit him or kicked him or something."

"Did you witness the abuse?"

"I didn't see anyone hit the dog, but I know it happened."

"What is your name, please?" the man asked.

"I—uh—I don't want to give my name," I said.

"Anonymous complaints are never given as much credence as those where we can check back with the complainant," he said. "Is this Pat Larson?"

After a second of stunned silence at hearing my mom's

name, I realized that the sheriff's department would have caller ID. He knew what telephone number I was calling from.

"Pat Larson is my mom," I said, "but she'd take away my allowance for a year if she knew I was calling you, so please don't tell her."

The man's voice softened. "I'll have someone check on the dog," he said, "but it's difficult to prosecute a cruelty case without an eyewitness." I was pretty sure Andrew was right, and this wouldn't be top priority on this man's to-do list. Probably he would pass my message along to Heidi Kellogg.

After I hung up I wished I hadn't called. I really didn't want the sheriff or anyone else to go get Ra. I wanted to rescue him myself. I wanted to bring him home and take care of him and know he was safe.

I wished we'd gone back with the leash on Friday, after Ra let us pet him. We could have rescued him right then, instead of waiting. At the time we had agreed we should wait another few days, to be sure that Ra would go with us on the leash. If we'd known what was going to happen Saturday night, we would never have waited.

Well, I told myself, *there's no sense second-guessing yourself now. The important thing is to get Ra away from there as fast as possible. A rapid, remarkable rescue.*

I went back again late in the afternoon, at the usual time, taking Ra's food and water. As I rode my bike toward Ra's street, I thought, *what if he's gone again?* What if he's not on the chain? What if he's inside? Would I have the courage to knock on that door?

Ra was there. He stood when he saw me, moving slowly as if it hurt to put weight on his legs. He acted hungry but ate only half his food, then lapped a little water.

At least he's standing now, I thought. *He has to be able to walk from here to the fort tomorrow. We have no other way to get him there.*

Andrew called as soon as he got home from his grandparents' house. He was as outraged as I was over Ra's condition. "Crummy, cruel clod," he said.

We whispered into the phone, making our plans for the next day. As soon as Ra finished eating, I would unclip the chain and remove the metal choke collar. Next we'd buckle the soft new sun collar around his neck and snap the leash on. Then we would lead Ra away from his captor and into his happy new life.

Thinking about it in bed that night, I had so much excited, nervous energy that I felt I might explode. My thoughts bounced up like popcorn in a microwave. What if someone saw us? What if Ra got scared and bolted and we couldn't control him? What if he howled at night because he didn't like to be alone in the fort, and Mom heard him? All the things that could possibly go wrong raced through my mind.

I never considered backing out of our plan, though. I couldn't let my dog spend his life hungry, afraid, and chained to that tree. I couldn't let him spend another night inside Mean Man's house. If Andrew and I didn't save Ra, who would? Tomorrow, Ra would be mine for real, not just in my mind.

CHAPTER SIX

I was late to school on Monday because I had an appointment at the orthodontist. Mom dropped me off at school afterward. As I crossed the entry hall and started to turn the corner toward the office with my signed excuse, I saw Gerald next to the bin where we were collecting supplies for the puppy mill dogs. He was bent over the bin, with both hands inside it. I stepped back, then peered around the corner, watching him.

When he stood up he had a can of dog food in each hand. He stuffed the cans in his backpack, then reached into the bin again. My jaw dropped. Gerald was stealing the donated dog food!

I burst around the corner and hurried toward him. "Hey!" I yelled. "Get away from there!"

Gerald quickly straightened up and turned to face me. He had a fake grin on his face. "What?" he asked, all innocent.

"Put back the dog food you stole," I said.

"I didn't steal anything."

"Yes, you did! I saw you take two cans out of the bin and put them in your backpack."

Mrs. Vargus, who works in the school office, came into the hall. "What's going on here?" she asked.

"He's stealing dog food out of the donation bin," I said.

"I was putting dog food *in*," Gerald said.

"I saw him! He was bent over, with his hands in the bin, and then he stood up and put two cans in his backpack."

"You don't know what you're talking about," Gerald said. "I brought dog food with me, and I'm donating it."

Mrs. Vargus looked at Gerald and then back at me. "This is a serious accusation, Rusty," she said. "Are you sure you want to make it?"

I thought of the consequences of being a tattletale. I realized that, just as I had no proof that Ra was mistreated, I had no proof that Gerald had stolen the dog food. It was my word against his. But I was too angry to back down.

"Look in his backpack, if you don't believe me," I said. "You'll find the two cans I saw him take."

"You'll find the cans I hadn't dropped in the bin yet," Gerald said.

Mrs. Vargus sighed. "I think you both need to talk to Mr. Burbank," she said. As we followed Mrs. Vargus toward the principal's office, Gerald whispered, "You're going to regret this."

Mrs. Vargus pointed to a row of chairs outside the principal's office. "Wait here," she said.

While we waited, I glared at Gerald. "Stealing donated dog food that's meant for mistreated animals is about as low as it gets," I said.

"You don't know half as much about this as you think you do," he replied.

"What is there to know? I caught you stealing, and now you're lying about it."

Before Gerald could respond, Mr. Burbank called me into his office and had me tell my version of what had happened. Then he had me wait while he talked alone with Gerald. At the end of that, he talked to both of us together.

"There is no way for me to know for certain which of you is telling the truth. Rusty, I see no reason why you would make up such a story, but you can't prove it, either. Gerald, I'm giving you the benefit of the doubt. I want you both to go to class now, and I trust that there will be no more incidents regarding stolen dog food." He looked at me. "Also, there will be no discussion of this with your classmates."

Gerald smirked.

I couldn't believe it. Once again, Gerald was getting away with no consequences for his misdeeds.

As we left the office to go to Mrs. Webster's classroom, Gerald made a big show of taking the two cans of dog food out of his backpack and putting them in the bin.

"It would have been faster if you'd let me do that to begin with," he said.

"I know what I saw."

During recess I told Andrew what had happened. He was as furious as I was. "We should tell Mrs. Webster," he said. "We should tell the whole class."

"Mr. Burbank specifically said I can't tell anyone. I shouldn't even be telling you."

"It isn't fair," Andrew said. "Gerald never gets punished."

"You got that right."

The classroom clock seemed to tick in slow motion. As the minutes dragged by, all I could think was, *Today is the day we rescue Ra! Today is the day I have a dog of my own.* Well, mine and Andrew's, but the fort where Ra would live was next to my house, and I'm the one who found Ra to begin with so it seemed as if he were mostly mine.

I didn't mind sharing him with Andrew. Without Andrew, I would not have had the nerve to rescue Ra. Also, Andrew had split the cost of the blanket and bowls with me, and he had provided the collar and some canned dog food to supplement the dry food.

The only time I really paid attention that morning was when we worked on our plans for helping the puppy mill dogs. "On Friday," Mrs. Webster told us, "we're going on a field trip to the Humane Society." When the cheering died down, she continued, "We'll see some of the rescued dogs, and we'll deliver all of the food and supplies that we've collected."

"Will we get to pet the puppies?" Lexi asked.

"I don't know. The puppy mill owner signed over custody of all the dogs to the Humane Society. Some of them will be released for adoption on Saturday."

More cheering erupted. Mrs. Webster had to whack her ruler against the edge of her desk to get us to quiet down. "This afternoon, we will give short talks to the other classes, to remind them to bring their donations by Friday." We spent the rest of the morning working on our speech for the other classes. When it was written, each of us learned the talk and we practiced giving it to one another.

After lunch, we went in groups of six and made our presentations.

When our time for working on the puppy project ended, my mind drifted away from my lessons and back to Ra. I kept thinking, *Today's the day.*

I rushed home from school, took the books out of my backpack, and put in dog food and one of the pans. I didn't take water this time, since Ra would soon be back in the fort where he'd have fresh water any time he wanted it.

I stopped in the kitchen to grab a couple of cookies and

saw a note from Mom. *I'll be home early today, so stick around after school. You need a haircut.*

Oh, no! She could arrive at any moment and I'd never talk her out of taking me to get my hair cut. I would have to pretend I hadn't seen the note. I jammed the cookies in my pocket and rushed out the door, nearly colliding with Andrew on the front step.

"We have to get out of here," I said. "Mom's on her way home and wants me to get a haircut."

Andrew turned around and ran away from my house, heading toward Ra's street. That's one thing I like about Andrew. He never needs a long explanation. If I say we need to go, he hightails it out of there.

It would have been faster to ride our bikes to Ra's house, but we had agreed to walk today because once we had Ra on his leash, we wouldn't want to deal with bicycles. Instead of walking, we ran.

By the time we reached Ra's yard, my heart was racing—not because we had run too fast but because I was so excited. Ra saw us coming and wagged his tail. He seemed better. I fed him, as I always did, but instead of watching him eat I looked nervously around, checking to see if any cars were approaching or any neighbors were watching out their windows.

As Ra licked the pan, making sure he got every scrap, Andrew said, "Okay, let's do it."

I curled my fingers around Ra's collar and tried to remove the chain, but the clasp was rusty, and I couldn't get the chain unclipped.

"Hurry!" Andrew said as he picked up the empty food dish.

"I'm trying. The chain is rusted; it won't open. I can't get it off his collar and with the chain on, the collar won't loosen enough to take it off."

"He was unchained Saturday night, when he was inside."

"Whoever unhooked him was way stronger than I am. You try."

Andrew tried. He couldn't get the chain unclipped, either. "We need to spray it with WD-40," he said. "That's what my dad uses when our gate hinges get rusty."

"It will take too long to go to your house to get WD-40."

We stared at each other. "Do you have any money with you?" I asked.

"I have five dollars."

"Let's try the store."

We ran to the nearby convenience store, where I had bought Ra's hot dog that first day, but they did not carry WD-40. Instead we bought a small bottle of vegetable oil. We hurried back to Ra and doused his rusty collar with vegetable oil. I rubbed the oil on the clip that attached the chain to the collar.

"If we get the chain off," Andrew said, "let's just hook the leash to the collar he has. We can switch to the new collar when we get him home."

My hands were soon a greasy mess. The rust came off on them, turning my fingers orange. I rubbed more oil on the clip, then tried opening it, and this time it unhooked.

Andrew quickly snapped the new leash on Ra's collar while I wiped my hands on my jeans.

"Come on, boy," Andrew said.

Ra hesitated.

"It's okay, Ra," I told him. I put one hand on his side and petted him. "You're going to live in the fort now, and we'll take care of you."

We walked slowly away from the tree, and Ra followed us. When we reached the sidewalk, we picked up the pace. Ra trotted beside us and never once looked back at the yard where he had been held captive.

When we reached my street, we peered anxiously around. My neighborhood was not like Ra's. People were often out in their yards, pulling weeds or pruning. If any of my neighbors saw me with a dog, the word was sure to get back to Mom. Luckily, I didn't see anyone.

We headed into the greenbelt and unlocked the door of the fort. Ra marched right in, as if he knew this was now his home.

"We made it!" I said. Andrew and I fist-bumped each other.

Ra sniffed the milk crates and then pawed at the blanket. He turned around in a circle a couple of times before he plopped down on the blanket.

"My cousin's dog turns in circles like that, too," I said.

"It's a holdover from their wilder ancestors," Andrew said. "Wolves made dens in the tall prairie grass, or dug in the cool dirt on hot days. Dogs and wolves share ninety-nine percent of their genetic material."

I looked at Ra, wondering if he was part wolf. He didn't seem fierce enough for that. My cousin's dog was a Chihuahua, which seemed even less likely to be a descendant of wolves, but I did not doubt Andrew's facts.

Andrew had brought an old towel to the fort to use on Ra's paws if it rained. I wiped my hands on it and then used it to clean as much of the oil off Ra's fur as I could. I took off the choke chain, and Andrew buckled the sun collar around Ra's neck.

"That looks great," I said. I sat on the floor next to Ra, stroking his side. He gave a contented sigh and put his head on my leg. I couldn't stop smiling.

"We need to decide on a story," Andrew said.

I waited for him to explain.

"In case someone sees Ra and asks about him, we need to be able to explain where we got him and why we're keeping him in the fort. We both need to have the same story."

I didn't even want to think about anyone discovering Ra, but I knew Andrew was right. "We can say we found him," I said.

"No," Andrew said. "If we found him we should have tried to find out who lost him. We would have posted flyers and let people know we had found a dog. We need a believable story of why he's really ours."

"Some kids gave him to us in front of the grocery store," I said. "We had gone to buy potato chips and there were these two girls standing out in front with Ra, asking every shopper if they wanted a free dog. We said yes."

Andrew nodded. "Perfect," he said. "I've seen people there before with puppies or kittens. It's a stupid way to find a home for an animal, but it does happen. It's believable."

"One girl was about ten," I said, "and the other was maybe seventeen or eighteen. They said their family was moving out of state and couldn't take the dog and they didn't want their parents to turn it in to a shelter. They wanted to be sure he went to someone who would love him, and we promised that we would."

"I didn't know you could lie so well," Andrew said. He seemed truly impressed. "No wonder you always get A's in language arts. You tell lively, lavish lies."

"What lies?" I said, trying to look innocent. "I'm merely telling you where I got Ra."

"The girls told us his name was Max," Andrew said, "but we decided to change it to Ra."

"Yep," I agreed. "That's exactly what happened."

"We're keeping him in the fort because we want to share him," Andrew said. "This way we can take turns walking him and feeding him, and he belongs to both of us."

I nodded. Although I secretly felt Ra was more my dog than Andrew's, I knew that wasn't really fair.

A voice called from beyond the trees. "Rus-ty!"

"Uh-oh," I said. "That's my mother. I'd better get home before she decides to look here for me."

"I'll stay awhile," Andrew said. "When I go, I'll take his old collar and the bottle of oil and put them in the trash can by the ball field."

"Good thinking," I said. "I'll come back and walk him before I go to bed." I gave Ra a quick pat on the head and hurried toward home.

"There you are," Mom said when I walked in. "Where were you? Didn't you see my note?"

"Note?" I said.

She pointed to the note she had left me. I picked it up, as if I were reading it for the first time. "Sorry," I said. "I went for a walk."

"Well, it isn't too late to get your hair cut," Mom said, "if we leave right now."

I grabbed two more cookies.

"What on earth did you get on your jeans?" she asked.

I looked at the oily orange streaks, shrugged, and followed her out the door.

After dinner that night, while Mom watched *Wheel of Fortune*, I slipped quietly out the back door. Mom's a fan of both *Wheel* and *Jeopardy!*, so I had an hour to be with Ra. As long as I was back home before *Jeopardy!* ended, Mom would not miss me.

Ra whined excitedly when he heard me unlock the padlock. When I stepped inside, he pranced around, whacking my legs with his tail. I petted him, gave him a dog biscuit, and then snapped the leash on and took him outside. I stayed in the trees nearby, nervous that if I set off down the sidewalk with Ra someone I know would see us. Eventually, I knew he would need more strenuous exercise, but for tonight we walked around close to the fort while he sniffed and marked the territory as his own.

After I took him back inside the fort, I sat beside him and petted him awhile. I burrowed my face into the fur on his neck and inhaled the doggy smell. I laid my cheek against him. "You'll sleep here tonight, Ra," I told him. "I'll be back to take you out tomorrow morning."

I wished I could bring my sleeping bag to the fort and sleep with him. Better yet, I wished he could come inside with me and sleep on my bed.

I set my alarm to go off half an hour earlier than usual, but I'm a zombie in the mornings. I staggered around, staring at my clothes as if unsure what I was supposed to do with them. I ended up having only ten minutes with Ra—barely long enough to take him outside. I put some kibble in his bowl and promised to be back as soon as I got home from school.

"Don't bark while I'm gone," I warned him. "You have to be quiet so nobody discovers that you're here."

CHAPTER SEVEN

A deadline for bringing their donations had spurred the other classes into action. That day as we emptied the bins and counted the contents, someone called the pile of blankets and towels "Donation Mountain," and the name stuck.

My class's creative project group had made dog and cat place mats. They drew animal pictures on 8 x 14 paper, and then Mrs. Webster had laminated the drawings. They were perfect for putting under pet food and water bowls. The kids in that group decided to charge three dollars each, and if I'd had three dollars I would have bought one to put under Ra's bowls.

Many teachers purchased place mats as soon as they saw them. The group had set up a card table at the high school basketball game and had sold out of the place mats in less than twenty minutes. They had earned one hundred fifty dollars to give to the Humane Society! The class got so excited over being able to donate toward the rescued dogs' veterinary care that we asked the group planning a bake sale if all of us could participate.

The afternoon before the bake sale, Andrew and I walked Ra after school but instead of playing with him after his walk, we put him back in the fort while we went to Andrew's house to bake cookies. We made a double batch of peanut butter cookies and a double batch of chocolate chip cookies. Then we stirred up some Rice Krispies Treats.

Wendy the Whiner hung around, but we told her she could only watch.

"I want to stir the dough," Wendy whined. "I want to scoop it onto the cookie sheets."

We said it was a school requirement that nobody except kids in Mrs. Webster's class could help bake for the bake sale.

"You and I can bake cookies tomorrow," Andrew's mom said. "Today the boys are going to do it."

"That isn't fair. Andrew always gets to do everything first. He gets to go bowling."

Andrew rolled his eyes. "I take you along, don't I?" he said. "Rusty and I let you come with us every Saturday afternoon."

"But I don't get to throw the ball."

"That's because it's too heavy for you," Mrs. Pinella said. "And the special shoes that the bowling alley requires are too big for your feet. You're lucky the boys let you go along to watch, so stop complaining."

While the cookies cooled, we went back to the fort. Ra got so excited to see us that he spun in circles. We took him outside and threw his tennis ball for him. Then we gave him a rawhide chew bone to keep him occupied while we went back to Andrew's house to pack the cookies.

Andrew and I had made twelve dozen cookies. "That should bring in a lot of money to help the dogs," he said as we looked at the plates lined up on Andrew's kitchen counter.

"A copious cookie contribution," I said.

"Copious minus two," Andrew said as he handed me a cookie and bit into another one himself.

We had sturdy paper plates and put a dozen cookies on each, then covered them with plastic wrap.

We beamed at each other, feeling good about our afternoon's work. We even remembered to thank his mom for contributing all the ingredients and letting us use her kitchen.

"I'll drive you to school tomorrow," Mrs. Pinella said. "We'll pick you up, Rusty, so you can help carry the cookies."

The bake sale was a success. Parents and grandparents stopped to purchase goodies. Mom gave me five dollars that morning and told me I could choose something to put in the freezer to have for my lunches. I bought two dozen of the cookies that Andrew and I had baked.

Mrs. Webster bought a cake, and most of the other teachers bought baked goods, too. By the time I got on the bus to go home that day, everything had been sold. Before we left for the Humane Society field trip the next morning, Mrs. Webster announced that the bake sale had raised one hundred eighty-six dollars. When we added the cash donations to the place mat and bake sale money, our class had a total of five hundred eighteen dollars to help the dogs!

When we got to the Humane Society, we each carried in a box or bag filled with food, towels, or blankets. The parents who had come along carried in the rest of our donations. Mrs. Webster introduced Mr. Buckingham, the director of the Humane Society, and presented him with a check for five hundred eighteen dollars. We posed for a picture with Mr. Buckingham, and then he and two volunteers gave us a tour of the shelter.

First we walked down a long hallway that had glass along one side. On the other side of the glass, cats of all sizes and colors awaited adoption, in individual cages. Each had a dish of food and water and a small box of cat litter. Some of the cats used their litter boxes as beds. A few cats had red-and-blue knit blankets, just the right size for a cat to curl up on.

Several put their noses to the glass, as curious about us as we were about them. Others eyed us cautiously. Some slept through our visit. Each cat's window had a number on it. Pieces of paper with corresponding numbers were pinned to the wall on the opposite side of the hallway. Those papers told how old the cat was, its name, and anything known about its background.

I saw a particularly cute calico and wished the glass wasn't there so I could pet it. The paper for that number said, "Buttons. Spayed calico female, approximately three years old. Good with dogs, other cats, and kids. Family is moving and can't take her."

When Mr. Buckingham asked if there were any questions about the cats, I raised my hand. "Buttons seems like a great cat, but it says her family is moving and can't take her," I said. "Why wouldn't they take her?"

One of the volunteers muttered, "Good question," as if she had wondered the same thing herself.

"People have many reasons for leaving a cat with us," Mr. Buckingham said. "Even when their reason doesn't seem very good to me, I'd still rather they brought the animal here than to dump it somewhere. At least here Buttons is safe and has food and will have a chance to get a permanent home."

He had not actually answered my question, but I didn't say anything else. It must be really hard to work in a place like this and stay patient with the reasons people give for not keeping their pets.

Next we went to the dog area. It was a huge room containing several rows of kennels, each about six by eight feet big with a heavy wire gate across the front. A few dogs had blankets but most had only the bare concrete floor. I was happy that we'd brought so many blankets. Donation Mountain would help a lot of dogs.

"Usually," Mr. Buckingham said, "we have only one dog per kennel, but we've had to double up in order to accommodate all of the rescued dogs from the puppy mill." Three or even four dogs shared many of the kennels.

Most of the kids were oohing and aahing over the rescued puppies, but my eyes were drawn to a row of kennels that held big dogs. Several pit bulls watched me through the wire. Labradors, mixed breeds, and even a Great Dane pressed their noses against the wire gates as if saying, "Here I am! Choose me!"

When I saw a German shepherd, I approached that kennel. The dog looked so much like Ra that it could have been his twin sister. I read the paperwork that was clipped to the front of the kennel. "Female German shepherd, age two. Stray. Shy, but responds to attention. Spayed."

"Hello, girl," I said. "You're a pretty dog." She wagged her tail. I held my fist to the wire and she sniffed it. Andrew came and stood beside me.

"She looks like Ra," he said.

I nodded. "I'm glad we took Ra when we did," I said. "If the sheriff's department had rescued him, they would have brought him here, and there are already way too many dogs here."

Andrew let the German shepherd sniff his hand, too. "She probably doesn't have much chance of getting chosen with all those cute Westies and miniature schnauzers and dachshunds that are available from the puppy mill rescue," Andrew said.

"I wish we could take her," I said. "She'd be good company for Ra. Instead of being alone all day while we're in school, he'd have a friend."

"Maybe I could talk my parents into adopting her," Andrew said. "Then I could walk her over to your house and if anyone saw us with Ra, they'd assume it was this dog."

"But if your parents adopt her, she couldn't live with Ra, so she wouldn't keep him from being lonely."

"Oh. Right."

Gerald Langston came and stood next to us. I saw him read the paperwork on the German shepherd's cage. Then he leaned down, looking carefully at the dog.

"What are you looking for?" Andrew asked.

"I'm checking to be sure it's a girl dog, like the paper says."

"It is," I said.

"Why do you care?" asked Andrew, but Gerald walked away without answering.

"I hope he doesn't try to adopt her," I said.

Mrs. Webster told us it was time to return to the lobby,

where Mr. Buckingham would answer any additional questions.

Jordan asked, "How old do you have to be to volunteer here?"

"Sixteen," Mr. Buckingham said.

Hayley said, "How come some of the cats have little blankets and others don't?"

"Volunteers knit the blankets," he said. "When a cat gets adopted, its blanket goes along to the cat's new home, to help it feel secure. We always need people to knit more cat blankets for us."

"Are there specific instructions?" Mrs. Webster asked.

"I'll get them for you," one of the volunteers said, and she headed to an office.

Somebody wanted to know why the shelter charged a fee to adopt an animal. "Why can't you give them away, if it's a good home?"

"All of our animals are spayed or neutered before they leave," Mr. Buckingham explained. "They are vaccinated, wormed, microchipped, and given flea treatment. All of that costs money. The amount we charge for an adoption does not cover the cost to us of rescuing an animal. We depend on private donations."

By the time we boarded the school bus for the return trip, my head overflowed with information about the needy animals.

As we rode along I told Andrew, "I'm glad there are people who donate money to help homeless animals."

"So am I. When I'm old enough I'm going to volunteer here. It would be cool to be a dog walker or give tours of the shelter or sell stuff in their gift shop."

The Monday after the field trip, when Andrew came over after school, he knocked on my front door instead of letting himself in as he usually does. When I opened the door, he said, "I'm not staying. You need to wait until I'm back home before you go to the fort."

"What's going on?"

"I was followed."

I looked over his shoulder, my eyes scanning the sidewalk.

"Wendy is tailing me," Andrew said. "I think she's behind that big tree in Mr. Conway's yard."

I glanced across the street at the tree. Sure enough, something yellow stuck out from behind it.

"She's been bugging me for days," Andrew said, "asking what we do after school every day. She knows I come here because Grandma said something about it." Andrew's grandma stays at his house after school three days a week until one of his parents gets home from work. "I told her we're doing homework so she'd think it was boring, but you know Wendy. Once she decides she wants to do something, there's no stopping her."

"Sneaky, self-centered sister," I said.

"You got that right."

"So what are you going to do?"

"I'll go back home. I'm pretending I don't know she's following me. If she thinks she sneaked around and spied on me and nothing happened, maybe she'll quit asking to come with me."

"Okay," I said. "See you tomorrow."

Andrew nodded. Then he turned and started back toward his own house. I peeked out the window. When Andrew got to the corner, Wendy slipped out from behind the tree and followed him. I used to wish I had a brother or sister, but Wendy the Whiner has convinced me that it's better to be an only child.

I waited another five minutes. Then I hurried out to the fort to play with Ra.

The next afternoon Andrew and I went back to Value Village and bought a flat brush with narrow wire bristles. When we brushed Ra with it, we got lots of loose fur. The first time I brushed him, he acted nervous, but he quickly calmed down and seemed to enjoy the grooming.

We settled into a routine. As soon as we got to the fort in the afternoon, we took Ra out for a walk. Then one of us brushed him while the other one shook out his blanket and put fresh water in his bowl. After we fed him we took him out again and threw the ball for him, letting him run until his tongue hung out. I came back every night during Mom's TV shows and walked Ra again, even on the days when it rained.

Ra never once made a mess in the fort. I was certain he had not been housebroken—how could he be when he was always outdoors? But he always waited to relieve himself until Andrew or I took him outside. It was as if he felt so happy to have his own little home that he wanted to keep it clean. What a good dog! We kept an old shovel leaning against the fort and used it to bury Ra's waste so the area where we walked him and played with him stayed clean, as well.

Andrew realized two more times that his sister was following him. Both of those days, he made sure to lead Wendy in the wrong direction so there was no chance that she'd see me going toward the fort or, even worse, hear me playing with Ra in the woods. Each time, he called to explain why he couldn't come.

Then disaster struck. Andrew arrived as usual; we took the jug of water and the Baggie of kibble, and hurried to the fort. Inside, we greeted Ra and petted him.

It was Andrew's turn to walk Ra. He snapped the leash on, opened the door, and stood face-to-face with Wendy the Whiner.

CHAPTER EIGHT

I knew it!" Wendy cried. "I knew you were up to something."

My stomach felt as if I'd swallowed a stone.

Andrew glared at his sister. "You are not going to tell anyone about this," he said. "Not anyone!" His voice trembled with fury.

"That's what you think," Wendy replied.

"You little creep," I said. "Get out of here!"

"What do you want?" Andrew said.

"I want to come in. I want to be in your club."

"No way," I said.

"Then I'm telling Mom and Dad that you have a dog here."

Usually, I'm a nonviolent person. I don't like to watch fights in movies. I don't even like to watch wrestling on TV. But right then I would cheerfully have pounded Andrew's little sister with both fists except that I knew it would not solve the problem. It would only make things worse.

"Baneful, barbaric brat," I said.

Wendy's lower lip jutted out. "That's not allowed," she said. "Mom says threesomes have to be nice. They can't call other people names."

"There are exceptions to every rule," I said.

"You can't be in our club," Andrew said, "because we don't have a club. We're only taking care of a dog who needs a home. If you tell on us, he'll have to go to the animal shelter."

"That's right," I said, "and if he goes to the shelter he might not get adopted. There's not a lot of demand for big dogs. He might get put down."

"If that happens," Andrew said, "it would be all your fault."

I could tell Wendy was wavering.

"I want to help take care of him," she said.

Andrew looked at me.

"No," I said. I couldn't do it. It would take all of the fun out of having Ra if we had to share him with Wendy.

"Then I'm telling."

"Fine," Andrew said. "Go ahead. Be a baby tattletale, like you always are. But don't expect us to ever let you come anywhere with us again."

"That includes bowling on Saturday afternoons," I said.

Wendy burst into tears, turned around, and ran for home.

"Will she really blab on us?" I asked.

"I don't know. She might."

We took Ra for a quick walk, then sat in the fort to discuss what we should do.

"If she tells your parents," I said, "they'll call my mom. She wouldn't take Ra to the shelter. She'd make me take Ra back where we got him."

"Maybe not," Andrew said. "When our parents hear how Mean Man neglected him and hurt him, they might decide to let us keep him."

"Dream on. My mom has a thing about honesty, and that includes not taking something that doesn't belong to you."

I ran the brush through Ra's fur as we talked. Andrew shook out Ra's blanket and put fresh water in his bowl.

"I'm sorry about Wendy," he said.

"It isn't your fault. You tried to keep her from following you."

"That kid will be a private detective when she grows up."

"Or an investigative reporter."

"Grandma's at my house today," Andrew said. "If Wendy tells Grandma about Ra, there's a chance I can convince Grandma not to tell my parents."

"Unless Wendy tells your grandma and then tells your parents, too, when they get home."

"There is that possibility."

We looked glumly at each other. Finally Andrew stood up. Ra stood, too, wagging his tail eagerly.

"We might as well play with him," Andrew said. "It may be the last chance we get."

We threw the ball and Ra retrieved it. After about ten minutes, we gave him his dinner. Then we threw the ball some more. No matter how long we played, Ra was always ready for more. When it started to rain, we went back in the fort. Instead of sitting on our milk crates, we both sat on the floor beside Ra and petted him.

A knock on the door of the fort made both of us jump.

"Uh-oh," I said. "That's probably your grandma."

Andrew opened the door. Wendy stood there wearing her yellow rain slicker, so I knew she'd been home. Her puffy eyes and red nose indicated she had cried for a long time.

"What do you want?" Andrew asked.

"What does baneful mean?"

I glared at her.

"Look it up," Andrew said.

"I didn't tell," Wendy said.

"Lucky for you," I muttered.

"So, what do you want?" Andrew repeated.

"I want to keep going bowling with you."

"On one condition," Andrew said. "As long as you don't tell anyone about this dog, *and* you don't come over here and bug us, we'll keep taking you on Saturdays whenever we go bowling."

"I don't bug you."

"Yes, you do," I said. "You sneak around and follow Andrew and spy on us. That has to stop."

"There's no law that says I can't come over here."

"Maybe not," I said. "But *we* say so. Think about the Saturday bowling and all the times we let you watch a movie with us and take you to the park and push you on the swings. If you want all that to keep happening, you have to leave us alone unless you're specifically invited."

"You're not nice," Wendy said. "I don't like you."

I clamped my mouth shut to avoid saying, "I don't like you, either." I didn't want to make her so angry that she ended up reversing her decision and telling her parents after all.

"So, is it a deal?" Andrew said. "You don't tell anyone about the dog, and we keep taking you along for Saturday bowling."

"Bowling and going to the park and watching movies."

"Agreed," I said.

"Then it's a deal," Wendy said.

"Go home now," Andrew said. "When I get home, I'll play Candy Land with you."

After Wendy left, we sat with Ra for a while longer. "I think we're safe," I said.

"For now."

"She wants to hang out with us more than she wants to squeal about Ra."

"That's what she says, but Wendy has never in her life been able to keep a secret. The first time she's mad at me for anything, I'm betting she spills the whole story."

I hoped Andrew was wrong, but he knew his sister better than I did.

CHAPTER NINE

It took only three days for Andrew's prediction to come true. Instead of going bowling on Saturday afternoon that week, Andrew and I decided to take our skateboards to the skateboard park. It was unusually warm for November, and we had spent our money on flea treatment for Ra and couldn't afford bowling. Who knew that good flea treatment was so pricey?

After we put it on Ra and played with him, we went to Andrew's house for some lunch.

As we rinsed our dishes, Wendy arrived. "I'm ready," she said.

"For what?" Andrew asked.

"To go bowling. It's Saturday."

"We aren't going bowling today. We don't have enough money."

She looked at our skateboards next to the door. "Are you going skateboarding?" she asked.

"That's right," Andrew said.

"Then I'll go there with you."

I groaned. We were meeting Henry and Lucas at the park. We didn't need Wendy tagging along.

Mrs. Pinella came into the kitchen.

"I want to go to the skateboard park with Andrew and Rusty," Wendy said.

Mrs. Pinella raised her eyebrows and looked at Andrew.

"We're meeting some other guys there," Andrew said. "It would *not* be cool to have my little sister along."

"Not this time, Wendy," Mrs. Pinella said.

"But I don't have anything to do!"

"Don't be silly," Mrs. Pinella said. "You have more toys than Toys 'R' Us. You can set up your easel and paint."

"I want someone to play with!"

"Would you like to invite a friend over?" Mrs. Pinella asked.

"I don't have any friends," Wendy wailed.

I could see why.

"I want to go with Andrew and Rusty."

"There's nothing for you to do there," Andrew said.

"You can teach me to skateboard."

I groaned.

"No, I can't," Andrew said.

Wendy put both hands on her hips. "Then I'm telling Mom about the dog," she said.

I felt as if I'd been punched in the stomach.

"What dog?" Mrs. Pinella asked.

"The dog that Andrew and Rusty have hidden in their secret fort."

"Andrew?" Mrs. Pinella said. "Is that true?"

"It's a long story," Andrew said.

"I have all day," Mrs. Pinella replied.

Andrew told his mother the story we had agreed on. He said we were given the dog by two girls at the grocery store. I backed him up with details.

When we were done, Mrs. Pinella said, "I have to tell your mom about this, Rusty. You know that, don't you?"

I nodded.

"Is she home?"

I nodded again.

"I'll call and see if she can come over."

While we waited for my mom to get there, Andrew and I went to his room. "Subversive sibling scumbag," Andrew said, but I was too upset to appreciate his threesome.

Ten minutes later Andrew and I were repeating our tale to my mother and Andrew's dad, who had returned from his run.

"When did this happen?" Mom asked. "How long have you had this dog?"

"Two weeks."

"This explains why you go for so many walks. You haven't been walking, you've been at the fort with the dog."

"I walk Ra," I said. "We take good care of him. We bought

dog food and a collar and a leash. We play with him and clean up after him."

"Why didn't you tell me about the dog?" Mom asked.

I looked down.

"Rusty?" she said.

"I knew you wouldn't let me keep him."

"So you deliberately did something that you knew I would not allow."

"So did you," Mr. Pinella said to Andrew.

"I can't believe you would do such a thing," Mom said. "How could you bring a dog home from the grocery store without any thought of how you would take care of him?"

Put that way, it did sound irresponsible.

I realized the story we had concocted was not as valid a reason for having the dog as what had really happened. I looked at Andrew.

He seemed to be thinking the same thing. "Should we?" he asked, and I knew he meant, *Should we tell the truth of how we got Ra?*

I nodded.

"That isn't really what happened," Andrew said. "We made up the story about the girls at the grocery store, in case anyone saw us with Ra, but that isn't really how we got him."

"Then suppose you tell us the true story," Mom said.

From the way she was glaring at me, I knew it had been a big mistake to lie about where we got Ra. We should have told the truth.

"Remember that day when I missed the bus and you drove me to school and we saw a dog chained outside in the rain?"

Mom nodded.

"That's the dog," I said.

"He was chained outside in the rain?" Mrs. Pinella said. She was clearly more sympathetic to this version than to us taking a dog at the grocery store. I told them everything—how I'd first noticed the dog, how thin he was, how he was chained all day in the sleet. Andrew chimed in with details as we told about feeding him and gaining his trust. The only part I left out was the ghost dog and how I had followed it in the middle of the night.

When Andrew and I got to the part about unchaining Ra and taking him away, Mom interrupted. "You *stole* someone's dog?" she cried.

"We *rescued* him," I said. "He'd been hurt."

"Stealing is stealing," Mom replied. "We'll have to take him back and apologize to the owner and hope he doesn't report you to the police."

"No!" I cried. "We can't take him back. The owner was mean to him."

"Are you sure?" Mrs. Pinella asked. "Did you actually see someone mistreating him?"

"No," I admitted.

"Ra was scared of us at first," Andrew said. "He acted as if somebody beat him."

"One day he was inside and then the next day he wouldn't eat, and he cried when I touched his leg."

I could tell Mr. and Mrs. Pinella were wavering, but Mom looked furious. "You can't take the law into your own hands," she said. "If someone's guilty of animal cruelty, there are agencies to deal with that. But you have no proof. You suspect the dog's owner was mean to him, but you don't know that for sure."

"I have pictures," I said. "I took a picture every day of Ra chained to the tree without any food. I kept a journal, too."

"A dog doesn't behave the way Ra did if its owner is kind to him," Andrew said.

"Andrew's right about that," Mr. Pinella said. "Perhaps we should talk to the people who own the dog. We can explain what happened and see what they say."

"What if they say we have to give him back?" I asked.

"It's their dog," Mrs. Pinella said. "If they want him back, you'll have to do it."

"Maybe they won't care," Andrew said. "Maybe they were glad to be rid of the responsibility of a dog, and they'll say we can keep him."

"If they don't, we could offer to buy him," I said.

Mom looked as if I had suggested we purchase a dozen alligators. "We are *not* buying a dog," she said.

"We could buy him," Andrew said, looking at his parents.

"I'll help pay for him," Wendy said. "I have four dollars."

"It's a little late for you to be helpful," I said. "It's your fault we have to take him back at all."

Wendy started to cry.

"Rusty!" Mom said. "You apologize to Wendy."

My mouth dropped open. "For what?"

"You made a little girl cry," Mom said.

"She bawls all the time," Andrew said. "What Rusty said was true."

"If Wendy hadn't told me now, I'd have found out sooner or later," Mrs. Pinella said.

"You can't blame Wendy for this situation," Mom said. "You got yourself into this trouble, Rusty. Now I want you to apologize for upsetting her."

"I'm sorry that you got your feelings hurt," I said to Wendy. "It will never happen again because I do not plan to ever talk to you again."

"That makes two of us," Andrew said.

Wendy ran out of the room.

Mom started to speak, but Mrs. Pinella gave her one of

those looks that adults give each other and shook her head as if to say, *Let it go. We can deal with this after we solve the main problem.*

"Let's go get the dog," Mom said. "We'll take him back right now."

Wendy had to stay home with her dad even though she pitched a fit because she wanted to go along. "Not this time," Mrs. Pinella said.

That was the only good thing that came out of the whole discussion.

Mrs. Pinella, Andrew, and I followed Mom out to the car and got in. She drove to our street and parked in front of the greenbelt. Then we all trooped through the trees to the fort and unlocked the door. Ra wagged his tail and did his happy dance, the way he always does when we come. He had no way to know that this time we were not going for a walk or out to play a game of fetch.

I snapped the leash on his collar. Mrs. Pinella let him sniff her hand, and then she petted him.

"He's a beautiful dog," she said. "I can see why you like him."

"He's a great dog!" I said. "It isn't just his looks. He's smart and friendly and loyal. He loves to play and . . ." All of a sudden, I started to cry. I couldn't help it. I stood there in the fort and bawled worse than Wendy the Whiner.

"Oh, Rusty," Mom said. "He *is* a fine dog—but he isn't *your* dog. It wouldn't be right to keep him."

"It isn't right to take him back to someone who doesn't feed him properly and leaves him chained to a tree all day, and hurts him," I replied. "A dog is a living being, not a piece of property. It would be different if I'd taken a computer or a jacket. Then you'd be right to make me return it. But a dog has feelings. He gets hungry and cold and scared."

Mrs. Pinella had tears in her eyes, and so did Andrew. To be fair about it, Mom looked none too happy herself. I don't think she really wanted to take the dog back, either, but she felt obligated to teach me not to steal.

"Let's get this over with," Mom said. She held the door of the fort open while Mrs. Pinella and Andrew went out. I followed with Ra. Mom closed the door behind us.

I didn't put the padlock on the door. Why bother? The only thing I cared about from the fort wasn't inside. He was on a leash, walking toward trouble.

CHAPTER TEN

As we approached the car, the collie's ghost materialized in front of us. She stood between me and the car door, as if trying to block my way. I looked at Andrew, who appeared not to notice anything unusual. I watched as Mrs. Pinella walked right through the ghost in order to open the front passenger door.

Andrew went around to the other side of the car and got in.

Ra, who had been acting uncertain, stepped ahead of me with his tail wagging, and sniffed noses with the collie. *Good,* I thought. *I'm not completely crazy if Ra can see the ghost, too.* Still, I wasn't sure what would happen when Ra and I got in the car. Would the collie's ghost try to prevent that? Did she sense where we were going and was trying to stop us?

"Get in, Rusty," Mom said.

I reached for the door handle. The collie's ghost eased out of the way. I let Ra jump in first, then I followed him and closed the door. I looked out to see what the collie did, but she had disappeared.

Ra seemed excited about going for a ride. He kept poking his nose at the window, leaving smear marks, and his tail waved back and forth.

I told Mom which way to drive. When we turned onto the street where Ra had lived, he quit wagging his tail and began to tremble. He left my lap and went to stand on Andrew's lap, then immediately came back to me. He started panting, his sides heaving in and out as if he'd just run a race.

"He's scared," I said. "He can smell where we are, and he's afraid."

"It's the house on the right," Andrew said. "The one back in the bushes." Mom slowed the car and turned into the driveway. Ra began to whimper.

"Look!" I said. "They got another dog!"

Mom stopped the car, and we stared out the window. A black Lab, about six months old, was chained to the tree where Ra had been chained. The puppy's fur was dirty. He watched us, but he didn't act happy to see us. He was listless, lying in the dirt.

As I looked at him, I froze. The puppy was not alone. Beside him, barely visible, was the collie's ghost. The ghost looked at us, alertly watching. I wondered what she would do if we got out of the car and approached.

"He doesn't have any food," Andrew said. "Just like Ra."

"Oh, my," said Mrs. Pinella.

"There's no water, either," Andrew said.

"No place for him to sleep," I added. "No doghouse for when it snows."

Ra sat on my lap. He kept shaking. He panted so hard that his tongue hung out of his mouth as he stared out the window.

"Look at Ra, Mom," I said.

Mom and Mrs. Pinella both turned in their seats.

"The poor thing is scared to death," Mrs. Pinella said. "I don't think we should make him get out of the car here."

"You want proof he was mistreated?" Andrew said. "Here's the proof."

I had my arms around Ra, trying to calm him, but he was beyond comfort.

Mom shifted the car into reverse.

"What are you doing?" I asked.

"We'll keep Ra," she said, "until I can call animal control and discuss the situation with them. I'll ask if there have been any complaints about this address."

"Even if there haven't been any," Mrs. Pinella said, "I'll make a complaint about the dog that's here now."

"It's okay, Ra," I said. "You don't have to go back."

"I'm not saying you can keep him," Mom said. "All I'm saying is that I'll look into the matter before we decide what to do."

As Mom began backing out of the driveway, an old clunker car came down the street. Dull blue patches, some dark and some light, shared space with reddish-brown rust spots on the car's exterior. The colors were uneven and random, like a tie-dyed shirt.

Mom waited for it to pass but it stopped and a man stepped out. He wore jeans and a T-shirt that had not recently been inside a washing machine. A tattoo of a snake curled around one bicep. When he started toward the car, Ra's lip curled back, baring his teeth. A low growl rumbled in his throat.

"Hey!" the man called as he pointed at Ra. "That's my dog!"

"Don't stop," Mrs. Pinella said. "Keep going."

Mom backed into the street, shifted into drive, and drove off.

"Hey, you!" The man ran after us. "Wait!"

Mom sped down the street. Andrew and I looked out the rear window as the man got back in his car.

"He's going to follow us!" I said.

Mom turned the corner, accelerated, turned again at the next corner. We made it back to Andrew's house without seeing the old blue car again.

"I didn't like the looks of that man," Mrs. Pinella said. "I'm glad we *didn't* knock on his door."

My heart was hammering as if I'd run down the street instead of riding in a car. "He's bad," I said. "You saw how Ra acted. That man has been mean to him."

"Yes," Mom said, surprising me. "I think you're right, but

that doesn't alter the fact that you went on his property and took something that belonged to him. Personal property laws protect everyone, whether they're nice people or not."

I didn't reply. Sometimes it's best to keep my mouth shut and let Mom think things over. If I argued now, she might feel compelled to defend her original position, but if she had time to ponder the problem, she might decide that there are degrees of right and wrong.

Mom dropped Mrs. Pinella at her house, but Andrew came home with me. We abandoned our skateboarding plan and spent the rest of the day with Ra. We wanted to make up for taking him to his old house and scaring him. We threw the ball; we gave him extra treats; we brushed him and petted him. We had always liked our time with Ra, but it seemed even sweeter now that we knew we might not be able to keep him. We wanted to make him as happy as we could, in case we had to give him up.

"What will you do if your mom says you have to take him back?" Andrew asked.

My stomach tied itself in knots when I thought about that possibility. "I don't know. I guess I'd have to do it. Either that or take Ra and run away, but I don't have anywhere to go."

"I think my parents would let me keep him," Andrew said. "Maybe they'll convince your mom to let us do that."

What I really wanted was for Ra to stay with me but if that

wasn't a choice, I'd rather have him be Andrew's dog than to go anywhere else.

"Did you see the collie's ghost?" I asked.

"No! Where was it?"

"First she was here, next to the car before we got in. It was as if she didn't want us to go. Then when we got to Mean Man's house, the ghost was standing by the new dog."

Andrew gave me his laser look. "Are you pulling my leg?" he asked.

"Honest, I saw the collie's ghost while we were walking to the car."

"Why didn't you tell me when you saw her so I could look, too?"

"In front of our mothers?"

I knew it bothered Andrew that I could see the collie's ghost and he couldn't, but I wasn't so sure that the ability to see a ghost was a good thing. I wasn't scared of the ghost, but I didn't understand why she kept appearing to me, either. I was already doing everything I could to help Ra. I had not wanted to put Ra in the car, even before the collie tried to prevent me from doing so.

Mom had called the city offices as soon as we got home but because it was Saturday, no one in the animal control department was available. Mom couldn't talk to anyone about Mean Man and the dogs until Monday.

That was fine with me. The longer we put it off, the better.

When Mom got home from work on Monday, she told me that she had called on her lunch hour and talked to someone in the city's animal control department. "They had a complaint for that address a few months ago," she told me. "A neighbor said a dog was left chained up with no food for days on end but when the animal control officer went to investigate, there wasn't any dog there. She contacted the person who had filed the complaint and learned that the dog had died the day before. She remembered the incident clearly because the woman who had called was so upset. She said it was a beautiful collie, and she blamed herself for not interfering sooner."

A collie. Mean Man had let a collie starve to death in his yard. Was that collie the ghost? Why would it stay around a place where it had been so unhappy? I didn't want to tell Mom about the dog ghost so I said, "Now what happens?"

"The animal control officer will go there and take a look at the conditions and decide if the Labrador puppy is being mistreated. She told me it is not against the law here to keep an animal chained for long periods of time, as long as it has food, water, and shelter."

"The puppy doesn't have any of those," I said.

"I told her that, and she promised to check it out." Mom heated some leftover enchiladas while we talked. I tossed a salad.

"Did you tell her about Ra?"

"No. I'm going to wait to see what she says after she's been to the property. It may be a day or two before I hear anything. City officials are not known for their speed."

"Andrew thinks his parents would let him keep Ra," I said.

"One step at a time," Mom said.

While we ate, Mom told me she had a Friends of the Library meeting that night. "You can come along, if you like," she said, "and do your homework at the library."

I shook my head no. "I'm almost done with my homework," I said. "I'd rather stay home and watch the football game."

"I won't be late," Mom said.

"Could I bring Ra inside?" I asked.

Mom hesitated. "I don't want you getting overly attached to him," she said. "If he doesn't go back to the man who owned him, he'll go to a shelter and be put up for adoption, or maybe he'll go to Andrew's house."

"He'd be company for me tonight while you're gone," I said. "We can watch the ball game together, and then he can sleep on the floor in my room. Only for tonight. Please?"

Mom sighed. "All right. Just for tonight."

"Thanks, Mom!"

I went out to the fort and snapped the leash on Ra. I walked him all the way around the block, to be sure he was empty. The last thing I wanted was for him to have an accident in the house.

I gathered up his blanket, his dishes, and his food. Then I led him through the trees and across my back lawn and into the house. As soon as I unhooked the leash, Ra began exploring. He sniffed everywhere. He found a stale piece of popcorn under an end table and ate it.

I filled his water bowl and put it in a corner of the laundry room where it wasn't likely to get accidentally kicked over. I showed him where it was, but he was more interested in smelling the rest of the house. When he got to my bedroom, he jumped up on the bed, turned in a circle, and plopped down. I swear he grinned at me, as if to say, "Finally! I'm where I belong!"

"You'd better not let Mom catch you there," I said.

I finished my homework and then went downstairs and turned on the ball game. Ra followed, and settled beside me on the sofa.

I was watching the instant replay of a missed field goal when I felt a blast of cold air. The ghost dog materialized in front of me. Ra lifted his head and then put it back on my leg. The collie acted upset. She paced over to the window, then returned to the sofa.

As I got up to go look out the window, the doorbell rang. When I walked to the door, Ra followed me. The collie quickly positioned herself between us and door, the same way she had when I was leading Ra to the car. I knew she did not want me to open the door.

The doorbell rang again, several times in succession. Whoever was out there didn't have much patience.

I have strict instructions never to open the door when I'm home alone unless I'm positive it's someone I know, so even if the collie's ghost hadn't come, I would have been cautious. There's a peephole in the door, and I looked through it.

A chill rippled down my arms. Mean Man stood on my front step!

He rang the bell again. I sat down on the floor with my back to the door and gathered Ra into my arms, hoping he wouldn't bark. If we stayed next to the door, Mean Man couldn't see us, even if he looked in the window. The collie stood beside us, staring at the door as if she could see right through it.

Mean Man pounded on the door with his fist. "Open up!" he hollered. "I know you're in there; I can hear the TV."

At the sound of Mean Man's voice, the hair stood up along the back of Ra's neck. He stared at the door and growled a low, throaty growl.

I leaned over him so his head was up against my chest. "Shh!" I whispered into one ear as I stroked his head.

The ghost leaned forward and head-butted Ra. Ra quit growling.

I shivered, feeling cold clear into my bones. Was it the collie's icy aura? Or was it my own fear?

Clunk!

I jumped at the sudden sharp noise. It sounded as if the man had kicked the door!

I wondered if I should stay where I was or if I should run to the phone and dial 911. Was Mean Man capable of kicking the door down? I was afraid if I let go of Ra he would bark, and Mean Man would know for sure Ra was here, so I sat still, holding Ra close and bracing myself for another clunk.

It didn't come. Instead, I heard footsteps stomp across the porch. Then a car engine started. I crawled to the front window and carefully peeked out. The old blue clunker pulled away from the curb in front of my house.

I reached down to pet Ra, who had followed me to the window. As I did so, I realized the ghost dog was gone. She had come to warn me about Mean Man and now that the danger was over, she had left.

My hands shook as I clicked off the ball game. How had he found us? He must have seen our license plate number when we left his house.

I opened the door and looked out, in case he had left a note, but there was nothing. *He'll be back*, I thought. *Now that he knows where we live, he'll be back.*

CHAPTER ELEVEN

I called Andrew. "Mean Man was here," I said. "He came to my house."

"What did he say?"

"I didn't talk to him. Mom's not home, so I didn't open the door. I saw him through the peephole. He pounded on the door awhile, and kicked at it, and then he left."

"Oh, man," Andrew said. "This is not good."

"No," I said. "It isn't."

"Do you want me to tell my parents? Should we come over there?"

I knew what Andrew really meant was that if I was scared to be alone, they would keep me company.

"Mom said she wouldn't be late. By the time you could get here, she'll probably be home. Besides, what can you do here?"

"Hold your hand?" Andrew said. "Help you be a fervently fearless fellow?"

"I'm okay," I said. "Ra's inside with me. Mom let me bring him in because she had to go to a meeting." I decided not to mention that the collie's ghost had tried to keep me away from the door. I knew it bothered Andrew that

I could see the ghost dog and he couldn't, so why bring it up?

"What did Ra do?" Andrew asked. "Did he bark? Did the man hear him?"

"Ra stayed by me but he didn't bark."

"Maybe he couldn't smell the man through the solid door."

"Ra knew who was out there, all right. He growled when the man yelled for me to open the door."

"Maybe he was too smart to bark and let the man know he was there."

"I held his head up against me to muffle the growling, and I petted him to keep him quiet." Talking about it made me feel better, and I started to relax. "I was a bodaciously brave boy," I said.

"The man must have traced your mom's license plate number. You can do it online for a fee."

"Don't say anything to your parents."

"You're going to tell your mom, aren't you? If he came once, he'll probably come again, so she needs to know."

"I'll tell her, but not tonight. I want to wait until she's talked to the animal control person. If I tell her now, she'll be spooked. I don't want her to give up Ra without a fight just because she's scared of Mean Man."

"Write down exactly what happened, with the day and

time, in that journal you keep about Ra," Andrew said. "If there's more trouble with Mean Man down the road, you need a record of when he was there."

"I will."

"And, Rusty?"

"What?"

"Be careful."

After I hung up, I felt restless. I left the TV off; the ball game no longer interested me.

I took Ra up to my bedroom and we sat on the floor together while I paged through an old comic book. Somehow I felt safer upstairs.

I opened the Ra folder on my computer, created a new document, "Mean Man," and wrote down the date and time that he had pounded on the door. I remembered what Andrew had said about more trouble with Mean Man down the road. I was pretty sure Andrew was right.

I decided to go to bed early. If I was asleep, or pretending to be asleep, when Mom got home, I wouldn't have to talk to her. It's uncanny sometimes how she can tell when something is bothering me even if I don't say a word. Mean Man's unexpected visit had rattled me and I didn't want to take a chance that Mom would pick up on my nervousness and start asking questions.

I needed to take Ra for his walk before I went to bed. For

the first time since I'd brought him home, I didn't want to put the leash on Ra and take him outside. What if Mean Man was parked down the street, waiting for us?

I went downstairs and looked out the window again. The street lamp in front of our house threw a pool of soft light onto the dark sidewalk. I didn't see Mean Man's car. I went into the kitchen and looked out that window, too. Then I snapped the leash on Ra's collar, grabbed a plastic bag and a flashlight, and led him out the door.

I took him into the trees around our fort. He was used to being walked there and we wouldn't be visible to anyone driving past. Even so, I kept listening for a car or, worse, footsteps. When the wind rustled the pine needles, I tensed and swung my flashlight in an arc behind me.

When Ra was finished, I led him back toward home. We were almost there, just beyond the circle of light from the street lamp, when a car drove down the street toward us. I froze as I watched it approach.

Andrew and I used to play a game on summer nights called Carlight Kill. Whoever saw the approaching lights of a car first yelled "Carlight Kill!" and the other person had to freeze in whatever position they were in and stay motionless until the car drove past. We had fits of laughter when we were stuck in an awkward stance. I wasn't laughing now.

Ra sniffed the grass, not paying any attention to my fear.

The car slowed as it came closer, and my heart beat faster, but my feet stayed glued to the sidewalk. Because I was looking into the headlights, I couldn't tell what sort of vehicle it was.

It continued past me and when the lights were no longer in my eyes, I recognized my neighbor Mr. Conway. He waved as he turned into the driveway across the street.

Back inside, I gave Ra a dog biscuit, showed him the water bowl again, and then went upstairs to bed. I made Ra stay on the rug beside my bed because I knew Mom would check on me when she came home.

By the time she did, my light was out. I heard her pause outside my door. She turned the knob and cracked the door open. Ra's tail thumped on the rug. I took deep breaths, pretending to be asleep.

As soon as Mom closed the door, I patted the bed beside me. "It's okay now, Ra," I whispered. "Come on, boy."

I felt safer with Ra stretched out next to me. I lay on my side, with one arm around him. As I inhaled his doggy smell, I hoped with all my heart that this would not be the only night I ever got to sleep with him.

At school the next day, Mrs. Webster handed out copies of the instructions for how to knit cat blankets. "If anyone wants to make these," she said, "you can bring them to me and I'll take them to the Humane Society cats."

For language arts we were supposed to write how we felt about helping the puppy mill dogs. Usually during writing time there's a lot of pencil sharpening and paper rustling and shifting about because some kids don't know what to say. That day, everyone settled down to write. It's easier to write when you have deep feelings about the topic, and all of us had come to care about those rescued dogs. Even Gerald wrote a paragraph without looking at someone else's paper first.

After school, I noticed the light blinking on the answering machine at home. We had two messages. While I bit into a piece of cold pizza, I pushed the *play* button to listen to the messages. The first was Mom's dentist's office, reminding her that she had an appointment next week.

The second one was Mean Man. "You have my watchdog," he said, "and I want him back." That was all. No phone number, no name, just, "You have my watchdog and I want him back."

The pizza no longer tasted good. I rewrapped it and put it in the fridge.

When Andrew got there, I played the message for him.

"I either have to erase this," I said, "or I'll have to tell Mom before she listens to it that Mean Man was here last night."

"Don't erase it," Andrew said. "You might want it as evidence."

"What? Do you think we're going to end up in court over Ra?"

"I only know this guy is not a good person, and you need to keep track of anything he says or does. Maybe you should put a new tape in the machine and save this one."

"I don't have another tape."

"It's interesting," Andrew said, "that he refers to Ra as his watchdog. Most people would say 'You have my dog.' It tells you why Mean Man got a dog—not because he wanted a companion, but because he wanted a guard for his property."

"What's to guard?" I asked. "The place is a dump."

We played with Ra, but it was not as much fun as usual because we both kept watching and listening for any sign of Mean Man. When Andrew left, I took Ra in the house with me. I did my homework and he lay on the floor with his head on my left shoe.

As soon as Mom came home I asked if she had talked to the person in animal control. "Yes," she said, "and it was interesting. She said she's had another complaint for that address. The owner's name is Myers. The animal control officer went there and found the black puppy chained up with no food, water, or shelter."

"Did you tell her about Ra?"

"Yes. She will investigate the owner for animal negligence

but she needs to collect more evidence. We're going to have Ra examined by a veterinarian tomorrow."

"He came here last night," I said.

"Who?" Mom dropped her purse on the table and stared at me. "Who came here?"

"The man we saw when we were going to return Ra. He knocked on the door last night while you were at your meeting. I looked through the peephole and saw who it was, so I didn't open the door. Before he left, he yelled and kicked the door."

"Russell Edward Larson!" I knew I was in hot water when Mom used my full name. "Why didn't you tell me this last night?"

"I was asleep when you got home."

Mom gave me her fishy look, the one that means she does not believe my story for one minute.

"You could have told me this morning."

"We were both in a hurry this morning."

"That's no excuse, and you know it."

I figured I might as well tell her the rest. "He left a message on the answering machine today," I said.

She walked to the kitchen desk where the answering machine sits and punched the *play* button. While the dentist's receptionist gave her reminder, Mom hit *erase*. Then Mean Man's voice filled the kitchen: "You have my watchdog and I want him back."

Mom closed her eyes and took a deep breath. She replayed the message and wrote it down.

I waited.

She did not erase his message. She took a piece of paper out of her wallet and dialed the number she'd written on it. I could tell she was listening to a voice-mail recording before she left her message. "This is Pat Larson. I talked to you earlier about the neglected dog on Woodson Street and the dog that my son took from that address. Rusty just told me that the dog's owner came to our house last night, demanding that we give his dog back. He also left a message on my answering machine today. Please call me when you get this message." Mom gave our phone number, then hung up.

"What's going to happen?" I asked.

"I don't know. It will depend on what the animal control officer says. Her name is Heidi Kellogg, and she was angry at finding the Lab puppy with no water or shelter. I think she'll pursue this."

"Heidi Kellogg? I talked to her when I first started feeding Ra. I called to report that Ra was neglected and Ms. Kellogg told me I needed proof. She said to call back when I had documented the situation."

"So you did try to go through proper channels," Mom said. "You didn't just jump in and take the dog."

I'd forgotten to tell her about that phone call, probably

because I was embarrassed that I'd made it without having an address.

"I started to do what she told me," I said. "I have a week's worth of pictures and journal entries, but when I saw Ra the day after he'd been inside, and I could tell he'd been hurt, I knew I couldn't wait any longer. I had to get him to a safe place."

Mom nodded. "You should have told me the situation," she said. "I would have helped you deal with it properly."

I looked at my shoes. "I know," I said. "I'm sorry."

Mom gave my shoulder a pat. "What's done is done, and the important thing now is to keep everyone safe."

I held my breath, fearing that she meant we'd be safe if we gave Ra back to Mean Man.

Thwack! Mom pounded her fist on the table.

I jumped.

"That man is not going to bully us into giving Ra back to him," she said.

"Go, Mom!" I said. "You rock!"

"We'll work with the authorities to see that Mr. Myers is brought to justice."

"I hope Mr. Myers goes to jail," I said.

"You'll need to be cautious," Mom said. "Don't walk Ra down the street by yourself. If Andrew isn't with you, wait until I get home."

The phone rang and I could tell it was Heidi Kellogg.

Mom told her the details of Mr. Myers's visit and phone message. She added, "My son has photos, taken a day apart, of
Ra chained to the tree. He kept a journal, too." She held the
phone toward me. "Ms. Kellogg wants to speak with you."

"Tell me about your pictures," Ms. Kellogg said.

I told her how I snapped a photo as soon as I arrived every
day. "On Saturday night, I took a picture of the empty chain
and of two cars that were parked in Mean Man's—I mean,
Mr. Myers's—driveway. That was when Ra was inside the
house," I said.

"Are they digital?" she asked. "Can you e-mail them to
me?"

When I said I could, she gave me her e-mail address and
asked me to send them right away. I gave the phone back to
Mom. Then I went upstairs, got out my camera, and logged
onto the computer. I downloaded ten photos. I hadn't looked
at any of them before because every time I took one, I was in a
hurry. Six of the pictures were almost identical, except for the
date. They showed Ra lying in the dirt, chained to the tree.
The photo of the two cars in the driveway and the one of the
empty chain were too dark, but if I looked closely, I could tell
that one car was the clunker with the dull patchwork finish.

I stared hard at the two photos of the collie's ghost. In the
one taken in my bedroom the collie was faint, but I could see
her in front of my bedroom door. I also saw the door, right

through her. The other collie photo, taken outdoors when she was standing beside Ra, was clearer. It showed two dogs side by side except that when I looked at Ra in the picture, I saw only Ra. When I looked at the collie's ghost, I saw the dog but I also saw the yard behind her.

I e-mailed all the pictures except the ghost photos to Heidi Kellogg. I also sent my journal as an attachment so she could read everything I'd written each day.

She responded almost immediately. "This will be helpful," she said. "I'll do everything I can to make sure Ra never goes back to where he was."

I looked at the ghost pictures again, feeling a tingle on the back of my neck. In the library books I'd skimmed, I had learned that when people take a picture of a ghost, it usually appears in the photo as an orb of light. One book had several pictures of bright round balls that looked as if they were lighted soap bubbles floating in the air.

The collie in my photos definitely wasn't an orb. She was a full-size dog with ears, tail, and fur. Maybe it's different with animal ghosts, I thought. Or maybe the difference is with me.

If the images I saw on my computer were transferred to prints, anyone who saw the prints should be able to see the collie's ghost. Maybe Andrew would be able to see her!

I highlighted the ghost photos, and hit *print*.

The printer was out of ink.

CHAPTER TWELVE

I called Andrew and reported the conversation with Heidi Kellogg. "She's nice," I told him, "and she really cares about Ra. She's compassionate, careful, and competent."

I thought it was a fine threesome, considering I made it up right on the spot, but Andrew didn't acknowledge my effort. I had the feeling that he wished he could have talked to Heidi Kellogg, too.

I didn't say anything about the ghost pictures. I didn't want to get his hopes up, in case he couldn't see the image of the ghost dog.

The next day while Andrew and I were walking Ra after school, Andrew said, "You'll never guess what Wendy the Whiner is doing." Without waiting for me to guess, he said, "She's knitting cat blankets for the Humane Society. She saw those instructions that Mrs. Webster sent home with us and asked what they were. I told her how some of the cats had these cute little blankets that volunteers had knit. Wendy got all excited and asked Grandma to teach her to knit, and now she's knitting blankets for the cats. She's already finished the first one. She used up some scrap yarn that Mom had, so it's all different colors. It's cool."

"That's a good project for her," I said.

"She's really enthusiastic about helping the homeless cats, and you know how she is—when she makes up her mind to do something, there's no stopping her."

I knew.

"Grandma brought her some more yarn today," Andrew said. "Wendy says she's going to knit enough blankets so that every single cat at the Humane Society has one, and when those cats get adopted, she'll knit more blankets for the next cats who come to the shelter. She's even going to buy more yarn with her allowance money."

It occurred to me that the same character trait that made Wendy such a pest might also make her a good volunteer for the cat blanket project.

Mom came home early because we had an appointment to take Ra to the veterinarian. Heidi Kellogg wanted him checked for any internal injuries or other signs of abuse. Mom said he had to be vaccinated, too. Heidi had recommended a vet.

The vet, Dr. Donna Taylor, made notes while Mom told her how we happened to have Ra in our care. Dr. Taylor weighed Ra and gave him a thorough exam. She listened to Ra's heart, checked his teeth, and felt his legs and stomach. "He is about two years old and ten pounds underweight,"

Dr. Taylor said. "He has a tender spot on his right haunch; I'd like to take X-rays."

Mom gave the okay, and Ra was taken to another room. Mom and I waited in the small exam room. "You realize this is going to cost a fortune," Mom said. It was not a question.

"I know." I couldn't offer to help pay because I had spent all of my money on Ra's blanket, leash, bowls, and flea treatment. I began to see why Mom had always insisted we couldn't afford to have a dog.

The vet's assistant brought Ra back. "He was a good boy," she told us. She gave Ra a treat. "Dr. Taylor will be in as soon as she's looked at the X-rays."

Ra wagged his tail when Dr. Taylor returned. He got another treat.

"Ra's right rear leg was broken at some point and it healed without being properly set."

I knelt beside Ra and put my arms around him.

"It doesn't appear to bother him now," Dr. Taylor continued, "but he might develop a limp as he gets older. The sore spot on his haunch is a deep bruise, probably the result of a blow with a hard object. A broomstick, perhaps, or maybe even a baseball bat."

Mom cringed.

"Oh, poor Ra," I said.

"This dog has clearly been mistreated," Dr. Taylor said,

"and if you need me to testify about this, I'll be glad to do so."

"Thank you," Mom said. "You may be hearing from the city's animal control officer. Her name is Heidi Kellogg. She referred us to you."

Dr. Taylor nodded. "I know Heidi," she said. "I've helped her with other cases and we both cooperate with the Humane Society to place animals in foster homes. I recommend that you apply as a foster parent. I can give you the paperwork, if you like. That way, Heidi could work to give custody of Ra to the Humane Society and, as soon as that happens, Ra could be officially placed with you for foster care."

I crossed my fingers.

"I'd like to do that," Mom said. "Thank you."

"Except for these injuries and being too thin," Dr. Taylor continued, "Ra is a fine, healthy animal. Let's give him his vaccinations and then all he needs is good food and some TLC."

"That's my job," I said.

Dr. Taylor gave Ra his shots, and her assistant brought Mom the foster home application. We took Ra out to the front desk. A man with a cat in a carrier went in to see Dr. Taylor.

I held Ra's leash while Mom got out her credit card.

The young woman at the desk handed Mom some papers.

"Here's his rabies certificate," she said, "and a printout of what we did today."

"How much do I owe you?" Mom asked.

"There's no charge for today's exam."

"But it was more than an exam," Mom said. "Dr. Taylor took X-rays and gave Ra his shots."

"I know," the woman said. "She never charges people who rescue animals. She says it's a way to thank those who do the right thing."

Mom's eyes filled with tears. "Thank you," she said as she put her credit card back in her purse. "Please tell her we're very grateful."

As we went out to the car, I was kind of choked up myself. Instead of a humongous bill to pay, we didn't owe anything.

Ra got in the backseat and stuck his head forward between Mom and me.

"Most people are good, Rusty," Mom said. "Remember that, and don't let the bad ones like Mr. Myers get you down."

"Ra behaved well, didn't he, Mom? He let Dr. Taylor examine him and he didn't even yip when he got his shots." I reached over to pet him, and he slurped my cheek. "You were a good dog at the vet's," I told him. "Good, good boy."

Our happy mood lasted until we got home. As we pulled into the driveway, Mom pushed the button to open the garage door, and then suddenly hit the brake. "Rusty!" she said. "Our front door is wide open!"

We both stared at the door. "I know I locked it," Mom said. "I remember turning the dead bolt."

She started to drive into the garage.

"Mom?" I said. My voice came out in a funny squeak. "The garage window is broken. There's glass all over the floor."

We stopped with the car half in and half out of the garage and sat there while Mom called 911 on her cell phone. "Someone broke into my house," she said, and then gave the address. "No, we have not gone inside yet."

When she finished the call, she said, "The police are on their way. They said not to go in because it's possible that whoever did it is still inside."

I thought they'd have to be pretty stupid to stay around when they heard the garage door open but then they'd have to be stupid to be breaking into somebody's house in the first place.

We only had to wait ten minutes for the police but it seemed to take forever. When they arrived, two officers went into the house and then a few minutes later they came back and said we could go inside.

"Keep Ra on his leash," Mom said.

I didn't know what to expect. I'd seen TV coverage of

burglarized homes, and they usually looked as if a tornado had ripped through the interiors, leaving drawers overturned and cupboards emptied.

Our house didn't look any different than it had when we'd left except for the broken window and the open door.

"Is anything missing?" one of the officers asked. "Usually, thieves take electronics first."

"We don't have much in electronics," Mom said. "Only the TV and the computer that's in Rusty's room." She pointed at the TV, then looked at me. "Go up and see if the computer's still there." It was.

"Small TV and old computer," noted the officer who had followed me upstairs. "Probably not what our friend was looking for. What about jewelry?"

Mom looked in the drawer where she keeps her jewelry box. "I have mostly costume jewelry," she said, "except for a pearl necklace that belonged to my grandmother." She opened the box. "The pearls are here," she said. "Everything else is, too."

We trooped back downstairs.

"Do you keep any cash in the house?" asked the officer.

"I hide fifty dollars emergency money in a coffee can in the refrigerator," Mom said. She looked; the money was still there.

We walked slowly through the rooms.

"In addition to the broken window," the officer said, "there's damage to the door frame." He pointed to the door between the garage and the house. "It looks as if whoever it was had a pry bar or some other tool to help get the door open. Then they left by the front door."

I shuddered, thinking about someone smashing our window, climbing through, and then prying our door open while we were gone.

"I don't think anything was stolen," Mom said.

"Whoever it was must have been looking for something specific," the officer said. "Either he found it and took it, but you haven't yet noticed that it's gone, or else he didn't find what he was looking for so he left."

"Maybe it was Mr. Myers," I said. "Maybe he was looking for Ra."

"Who's Mr. Myers?" the officer asked.

Mom went through the whole story of Ra.

"I'll follow up on that angle," the officer said.

After the police left, Mom called and left a message for Heidi Kellogg, telling her about Ra's checkup with Dr. Taylor and about the break-in at our house.

We swept up the glass in the garage and nailed an old tarp over the window. It wouldn't keep a person out, but it would help keep out the cold air.

"I'll call a glass repair place tomorrow," Mom said.

The door that had been jimmied didn't close properly, so we couldn't lock it, and that worried both of us.

"We're going to have to buy a new door anyway," I said, "so it doesn't matter if we put a few holes in it. Let's nail it shut."

I found three short pieces of board left from when we put bookshelves in my room. I nailed one side of each board to the door frame and the other side to the door itself.

"There!" I said. "It will take a bulldozer to get that door open." We had to use the front or back door and walk around half the house to get to the garage, but it was worth it to feel secure.

After we ate dinner, Mom filled out the application form to be a foster parent for the Humane Society. It was three pages long and asked questions such as *Do you plan to move soon?* and *Where will the foster pet be kept at night?* and *How many hours will the foster pet be alone during the day?*

Mom read each question out loud, and we discussed how to answer it.

When we finished, she signed and dated it. "I'll drop this off on my way to work in the morning," she said.

We were getting ready to take Ra out for his last walk when there was a knock on the door. Both of us gasped. Mom picked up her cell phone before she went quietly to the peephole and looked out. I knew she was prepared to call 911 if she saw Mr. Myers on our doorstep.

I gripped the edge of the table and watched. Mom still had her eye to the peephole. "Who is it?" she called.

"It's Heidi Kellogg."

I let out my breath and stood up.

Mom unlocked and opened the door. "Come on in. I'm Pat Larson, and this is Rusty."

"I got your message and I was in the neighborhood, so I decided to come in person instead of calling."

"Are you still working?" Mom asked. "I didn't expect to hear from you until tomorrow."

"Unfortunately," Heidi said, "cruelty investigation is an around-the-clock job."

She agreed that Mr. Myers might be the one who had broken in. "On Monday, I spoke with the neighbor of Mr. Myers who had filed a cruelty complaint against him last year about the neglected collie. She agreed to let me hide a video camera on her property. It's been taking surveillance video of the black Lab ever since. I picked up the camera a couple of hours ago; we now have proof that nobody gave the dog food or water for thirty-six hours, so I can charge the owner with negligence. I've already taken the puppy; he's at the Humane Society now and he'll go to a foster home tomorrow, as soon as he's been checked by a vet."

Mom showed her the completed foster parent application. "It says on the application that I'll need to attend an orientation session, and they're only held every two weeks."

"I'll talk to the Humane Society's director in the morning," Heidi said, "explain the situation, and have your application approved right away. You'll still need to attend the next orientation but we'll get Ra legally placed with you quickly."

"Do foster parents ever get to adopt the animals they foster?" I asked.

"One step at a time, Rusty," Mom said. "Right now, we need to be sure that Mr. Myers has no claim on Ra."

"That's right," Heidi said. "Of course, people like Mr. Myers don't pay attention to what's legal and what isn't. Even if we win a case against him and Ra is no longer his, he might still cause trouble."

Oh, great, I thought. *Mean Man Myers is going to be coming after Ra no matter what happens in court.*

CHAPTER THIRTEEN

Mom took the next afternoon off. She needed to be home when the repairman came to fix the window and install our new door, which was complete with a new dead-bolt lock. After he left, she went to the Humane Society to meet the person in charge of volunteer foster parents.

When I got home after school, Mom said, "It's official. Ra is now our foster dog."

I pumped both fists in the air and danced around the kitchen. Ra barked, and danced, too.

"I bought an ID tag for his collar," she said. "The Humane Society requires that all of their foster animals are microchipped. Usually they do it while the animal is at the shelter, before it goes to a foster home, but of course Ra wasn't with me. They said an ID tag is okay until we can bring Ra in to be chipped."

"Thanks, Mom," I said. "I know you never wanted a dog and it's nice of you to do this."

"Oh, Rusty," she said. "It isn't that I don't want a dog. It's that I worry about our expenses. Ra is a wonderful dog, but he eats a lot and he'll need more veterinary care. I can barely pay our bills as it is."

"Maybe I can get a part-time job," I said. "I'm old enough to do babysitting. I can hire out to shovel sidewalks."

"School is your job," Mom said. "By the way, Heidi Kellogg called. She's charged Mr. Myers with animal negligence. There'll be a hearing tomorrow afternoon."

Andrew didn't come that day to play with Ra. He said he had to clean his room, but I sensed that his room was an excuse, not the real reason. Although I had kept him informed of everything that was happening, I suspected that he felt left out. The situation had changed a lot in the last few days. Before Wendy spilled the beans, Andrew and I had done everything for Ra together. Now Ra lived inside at my house; Mom was Ra's foster parent; Mean Man Myers had come here; Heidi Kellogg kept Mom informed about the investigation; even the collie's ghost appeared to me but not to Andrew. Maybe it seemed to Andrew that he had helped rescue Ra but now he wasn't included any more.

I e-mailed him to tell him what Ra and I were doing, but he didn't reply. Then I e-mailed him the two ghost pictures. If he could see the collie's image, I knew he'd be thrilled. Still no response.

After I'd fed Ra and played fetch until he was worn out,

I put him inside with Mom while I rode my bike over to Andrew's house. We had been friends since kindergarten; I couldn't let anything come between us.

He seemed surprised to see me.

"Hi, Exalted Exciting Expert," I said. "I thought I'd hang out with you for a little while, if that's okay."

"Sure. I figured you were busy with Ra."

"He's sleeping."

"I just made popcorn," Andrew said, and I followed him to the den.

Wendy sat by the window, knitting. "Hi, Rusty," she said. "I'm making blankets for the homeless cats."

I fingered the soft green and tan blanket that dangled from her knitting needles. The large needles made big stitches, so the blanket was loose and porous. I imagined one of the Humane Society cats working his claws in and out of the blanket as he curled up on it.

"It looks as if you're almost finished," I said.

"Almost done with this one," she said. "I've already made seven others."

My jaw dropped. "This is the *eighth* cat blanket you've knit?"

"Yep. I like to make them and I want to help the cats."

"Here they are," Andrew said, pointing to a stack of blankets. Some were bright primary reds and yellows. Others were pastel pink and one was blue-and-white striped.

"They're beautiful," I said. "That's really great, Wendy," and I meant it. I never thought I'd be offering a sincere compliment to Wendy the Whiner but, as Mrs. Webster would say, Wendy had seen a need and was working hard to meet it.

"Did you get the pictures I e-mailed you?" I asked Andrew.

"I haven't checked e-mail since I got home from school. What did you send?"

"Let's look."

Andrew opened his laptop and we waited for the photos. Wendy put down her knitting and gazed over our shoulders.

The two pictures of the collie's ghost appeared side by side on the screen. "What's that dog's name?" Wendy asked.

"It's Ra," Andrew said. "You know that."

"No, the other dog," Wendy said. "The white one."

Andrew looked at me.

"She sees the collie," I said.

Andrew squinted at the screen, then shook his head.

"She's a funny-looking dog," Wendy said. "Are you going to rescue her, too?"

"We can't," I said. "She isn't a real dog."

"What do you mean? You took a picture of her."

"She's a ghost," I said. "She's a dog's ghost."

Wendy put her hands on her hips and cocked her head. "Are you trying to scare me?"

"Nope. I see the white dog, too, but I also can see right through her."

"I see through her, too," Wendy said. "That's why I said she's funny looking. I can see the yard behind her in one picture and something solid in the other."

"My bedroom door," I said.

"The ghost came to your room?"

"She wanted me to follow her. I think Mean Man Myers let her starve to death, and now she's trying to keep that from happening to any other dog. I believe she was trying to protect Ra."

"Oh." Wendy returned to her knitting. "Then she's a good ghost, and there's nothing to be scared of."

"That's what I think, too."

"Do you want to shoot some hoops?" Andrew asked. I got the feeling he didn't want to talk about the collie's ghost any longer.

"Okay."

He logged off. We got his basketball and went out to the driveway, where Andrew had a basketball hoop over the garage door. He dribbled the ball for a few seconds, then stopped and said, "It really bugs me that you and Wendy can see that collie, but I can't."

"It would bug me, too, if things were reversed, and I was the one who couldn't see the ghost. Maybe you're trying too hard. I'm never looking for her when I see her. She just appears."

Andrew shrugged. "Could be," he said.

"I was going to print the ghost pictures, to see if she'd show in them, but my printer's out of ink and I'm out of money. I'm a poor, penniless pauper."

Instead of responding, Andrew shot the basketball through the hoop. We played one-on-one for a while, but it wasn't as much fun as usual. Andrew didn't make up any threesomes and I felt as if we were only going through the motions of the game, without either of us caring if we played or not. I was relieved when Mrs. Pinella told Andrew he should get ready for dinner.

When I got home, I found a note from Mom: "Mrs. Gardiner needed a ride to her daughter's house. Back in twenty minutes."

Mrs. Gardiner has lived at the end of our block for fifty years. She can't drive anymore because her eyesight is too bad, so she sometimes asks Mom or one of the other neighbors for a ride.

Ra stood by the door, looking at me. I knew he wanted to go out. "We have to wait until Mom gets back," I told him.

He whined, and scratched at the door.

Mom hadn't put a time on the note so I didn't know when she'd be back.

Ra barked. He only did that when he really needed to go.

When I got the leash out of the drawer he came trotting over, wagging his tail. I snapped the leash on, and he tugged toward the door. He barely made it to the grass. "What'd you do," I asked, "drink the whole bowl of water?"

I turned to take him back inside, but he pulled toward the sidewalk. *Maybe he needs to go some more*, I thought, and decided to walk a short ways. As we walked, I thought about Wendy. When she told her mom about Ra, I was so angry at her that I had vowed never to talk to her again.

Now I had to admit it was a good thing that Mom and Andrew's parents had found out about Ra. He could be inside with me instead of being shut alone in the fort, and because of Mom, Ms. Kellogg was investigating possible cruelty charges against Mr. Myers. Mom was not only a foster parent for the Humane Society but she seemed to genuinely like Ra. None of that would have happened if Wendy hadn't told Mrs. Pinella that Andrew and I secretly had a dog.

Until now I had Wendy pegged as the most selfish kid in the world but here she was, knitting as fast as she could to help the homeless cats be more comfortable. Maybe I'd relent and tell Andrew that Wendy could come bowling with us the next time we went. If Wendy could change and become a kid who helped homeless animals, I could change my mind about letting her hang out with Andrew and me. Assuming, that is, that Andrew wanted to keep hanging out with me.

With my thoughts focused on Wendy, I wasn't paying attention to how far I'd gone, and I didn't hear the car approach. It wasn't until it stopped beside me that I glanced from the sidewalk to the curb and saw the mottled blue clunker.

Mean Man Myers sat behind the wheel.

CHAPTER FOURTEEN

I pulled in the leash so Ra was right beside me as I turned around. I walked faster, watching the car out of the corner of my eye. It rolled slowly down the street, keeping even with Ra and me.

I started to jog.

The car kept pace. Every few steps, I glanced at it, making sure the driver stayed inside. I had intended to stay in my own yard. How could I have come so far?

Mean Man Myers leaned toward the open window and said, "I came for my watchdog. You can put him in the backseat."

Ra growled when he heard the voice.

I kicked into gear and sprinted toward home as fast as I could run.

The car drove along beside me, belching exhaust fumes. Mr. Myers hollered, "You can't get away from me, boy. You stole my watchdog and if you don't give him back, I'll do more than ask politely. I'll take him!"

I kept running. My feet pounded on the sidewalk so hard that jolts shot up my legs. Ra loped beside me. He kept looking at the car with his ears flat. Once he barked but mostly he growled low in his throat.

I could see my house ahead. I wondered if any of my neighbors were home. Should I yell for help?

The blue car rolled along the curb next to me. "You hear me, boy? You don't give me my watchdog back, you're going to wish you had!"

I stopped running and faced Mean Man Myers. "The Humane Society took custody of Ra," I said, "because you didn't take care of him. They placed Ra with us and my mom is his foster parent. He is not legally your dog anymore and you have no claim on him."

"Is that so?" His eyes had a wild, unfocused look. "Well, I don't care what the Humane Society or anybody else says. I bought that dog fair and square, and he's my property. I don't take kindly to people who steal someone else's dog." He opened his door, stepped out into the street, and came toward me around the front of his car. He looked bigger up close than he had when he was sitting down. "If you keep that dog," he said, "someone's going to get hurt, and it won't be me."

I shot forward again. We were only a few houses from home now. Even if he chased us, I thought we could outrun him.

Mr. Myers didn't chase us. Instead he climbed back in his car, stomped on the accelerator, sped past us, then turned and drove up over the curb so that his car blocked the sidewalk. I had to run into the street to get around it. As I raced around the back of his car, he leaped out.

He was too close. I could tell I wasn't going to make it past him, so instead of continuing around the car I ran across the street and started up the front path to Mr. Conway's house. "Help!" I yelled.

Mr. Myers was too fast for me. He lunged forward and ripped Ra's leash out of my hand.

"Help!!"

Mean Man Myers gripped the leash in one hand and opened the passenger side door of his car with the other. He tried to make Ra get in.

Ra growled louder. The hair on the back of his neck stood on end, and his legs stiffened.

"Get in there," Mr. Myers said as he shoved Ra.

Ra refused to jump into the car.

"You'll get arrested if you take him," I said. "You'll be put in prison."

"They can't lock me up for claiming what's mine."

He leaned over, grabbed Ra around the neck, and tried to force him into the car. Ra bit him on the arm.

Mean Man Myers yelped, raised his arm to his mouth, and dropped the leash.

Ra took off down the street, with the red leash clunking along behind him. I hoped he would run home, but he galloped right past my house and kept going.

"Ra!" I yelled as I chased after him. "Come! Here, Ra! Come!"

But Ra seemed to have forgotten my efforts to teach him to come when called. He raced to the corner, turned, and vanished from my sight.

"Ra!" I shouted. "Come back!"

"You'll regret this, boy!" shouted Mr. Myers. "If you had given me my property when I asked, I wouldn't be on my way to the hospital; I'd be going home with my watchdog."

I ignored him. He wasn't hurt too badly if he could stand around yelling at me.

I knew I couldn't catch Ra on foot. I ran up our driveway, hoping Mr. Myers didn't come after me, and dashed along the walkway to the front door, relieved to see lights in the kitchen. Mom was home. We could take the car to search for Ra.

I pounded on the door with one hand and fumbled in my pocket for my key with the other, expecting to feel a hand on my back at any moment. Mom opened the door before I could get it unlocked.

I rushed inside, pulled the door shut behind us, and locked it.

"Rusty! What's wrong?"

"Ra is gone." I panted. "I was walking him, and Mr. Myers came and tried to take him. He grabbed the leash and tried to force Ra into his car. Ra bit him, and he dropped the leash, and Ra ran away. We have to go look for him!"

Mom rushed to the living room window and looked out. The blue car was idling in front of our house. Mean Man Meyers sat in it, staring toward our door.

"We can't leave the house while he's out there waiting for us," Mom said.

She turned off the TV news and called 911.

Hurry, I thought. *Ra is running farther away every minute. He could get hit by a car. He could get lost.*

Mom made sure all the doors were locked and then we went upstairs to wait for the police. We stood on either side of my bedroom window and peered out.

Mr. Myers was gone. A new fear rose to the surface of my mind: *Mean Man Myers could drive around and find Ra. He could still take him. Or he might be so angry that he would purposely hit Ra with his car.*

"We have to go look for Ra," I said.

"We need to wait for the police," Mom said.

"I'll go by myself. I can ride my bike."

"No. You're not going alone."

By the way she said it, I knew there was no point in arguing. The truth was, I didn't much want to ride around the neighborhood alone right then, anyway.

The same officer who had responded when the house was broken into came again this time. Mom explained what had happened and then the officer had me tell everything myself.

"You may have to get a restraining order against him," the officer said. "Meanwhile, if you find your dog, I wouldn't take him out of your own yard until this case is settled."

Mom gave me her *I told you not to go out alone* look and I knew I had it coming. Ra had needed to go out and then, once we were outside, I kept walking the same as I always did. What a bozo. I couldn't even think of a threesome bad enough to describe myself.

After the police officer left, I expected Mom to chew me out but she didn't.

Instead she said, "Let's go."

We drove slowly up and down the streets, going farther and farther from home. I kept my window down and called, "Ra! Here, Ra!" We did not see him.

When it was too dark to see beyond the headlights, Mom said, "I'm going home, Rusty. We both need dinner. Maybe Ra will come home on his own. If not, we'll look for him again tomorrow."

I looked hopefully at the front door as we pulled into the

driveway, but there wasn't any dog waiting for us. He wasn't at the back door, either.

While Mom fixed our dinner, I called Andrew and told him Ra was lost.

"We should make some flyers, with Ra's picture on them," Andrew said. "We can put them in store windows. I'll put a Lost Dog notice on Craigslist right away. If he hasn't come home by the time we get out of school tomorrow, I'll help you with flyers. We can use Dad's color copier."

After dinner, Mom e-mailed Heidi Kellogg and told her the latest development. I started my homework and Mom began opening the day's mail. I heard her gasp.

"What is it?" I asked.

Mom's hand shook as she handed me an official-looking letter from a law firm.

"Mr. Myers hired an attorney," Mom said. "He's suing us for stealing his dog."

"He can't do this!" I cried.

"I'm afraid he can."

"But he'll lose the case, right? You're Ra's foster parent now. It's legal for him to be here."

"It's legal now," Mom said, "but it wasn't legal when you took Ra. The dog was Mr. Myers's dog, and you stole him from private property. Every time you went there to feed Ra you were trespassing." She sounded tired, as if she'd like nothing more than to climb into her recliner and take a nap.

"What happens now?" I asked.

"I can't afford to hire a lawyer," Mom said.

"Maybe the Humane Society will help since they're responsible for Ra now."

"They're a nonprofit organization whose donors give money to save animals. They can't spend their funds on a private party's lawsuit."

"How can Mr. Myers afford an attorney?" I asked.

Mom shrugged. "Just because he lives in a rundown house and drives a beater car doesn't mean he has no money."

I went to the front door and called Ra. Then I called him from the back door. Where was he? All the horrible possibilities rushed through my brain like a flooded stream flowing downhill.

When I went back inside, I heard a muffled sound and looked in the kitchen. Mom's head rested on her arms, which were folded on the table. I realized she was crying. She had cried a lot in the first months after Dad died but since then no matter how short of money we were or how bad our troubles got, I never saw my mom cry.

The worst part was, it was my fault. I had got us into a huge mess, and I had no idea how I could get us out of it. I felt like crying myself.

CHAPTER FIFTEEN

I woke up twice in the night. Both times I went downstairs, opened the door, and called Ra. He didn't come.

I wanted to stay home from school the next day to look for him but Mom said I had to go. She called Mrs. Gardiner, who promised to walk past our house several times during the day and call Mom at work if she saw Ra. Of course with her poor eyesight, she wasn't likely to spot him unless he stood right in front of her.

Heidi Kellogg called while I was eating my breakfast. "The Humane Society is posting a five-hundred-dollar reward for information leading to Ra's safe return," she said. "They're using one of the photos that you sent me. Rewards have worked well in the past when they've sought information in animal abuse cases."

Mom drove me to school. We cruised slowly past Mr. Myers's house.

I don't know what we would have done if Ra had been chained in his old yard but he wasn't there. The dull blue spotted car was not in the driveway, either.

Andrew was waiting for me when I got to school. "Did you find him?" he asked.

"No." I told him about the reward and about driving past Mean Man Myers's house.

"If he isn't back by the time we get out of school," Andrew said, "I'll help look. We can put up flyers. Wendy said to tell you she'll help, too."

Whatever rift that had begun between Andrew and me was gone. Once again we were pals, working together, both on the same side.

"Let's tell Mrs. Webster and the rest of our class," Andrew suggested. "I bet lots of kids would look for Ra."

During the morning recess, Andrew and I stayed in the room. "Do you need something, boys?" Mrs. Webster asked.

"Can we talk to you?" I asked.

"Of course." She sat at her desk and motioned for us to sit in the front row.

"Remember the dog I wrote about that wasn't being taken care of?" I asked.

"The dog in your poem. Yes, I remember."

"Well, Andrew and I rescued him."

"How? What did you do?"

"We unchained him and took him home."

"Oh, my," said Mrs. Webster.

"We kept him hidden in our secret fort," Andrew said. "We fed him and walked him and gave him flea treatment and took really good care of him. We named him Ra."

"After the Egyptian sun god?" Mrs. Webster looked surprised.

"That, too, but mostly because *R* and *A* are our initials."

"Go on," Mrs. Webster said.

"Then my little sister blabbed to my mom about the dog," Andrew said, "and our parents were going to make us take him back, only when we got there, a different dog was chained up with no food or water, and Ra acted scared, so we didn't leave him there, after all."

"I should hope not," Mrs. Webster said.

"My mom talked to the city's animal control officer," I said. "The officer went there and saw the new dog. She took video of him for thirty-six hours, to prove he didn't get any food or water. She gave the Humane Society temporary custody of him and of Ra. My mom is Ra's foster parent, so Ra's staying with us. Then yesterday Mean Man Myers—"

"Who?" Mrs. Webster interrupted.

"The man who had chained Ra to the tree, Mr. Myers. He followed me while I was walking Ra and tried to take him away, but Ra bit him and ran off and now Ra's missing."

Mrs. Webster was quiet for a moment, as if it took a while to absorb all the facts we had given her. "Has Mr. Myers been charged with any crime?" she asked.

"Animal negligence. There's a hearing this afternoon."

By then the other kids were returning from recess. Mrs. Webster didn't say anything about Ra to them.

At lunch, Andrew said, "We should skip school this afternoon and go to that hearing."

"Are you nuts? Mom would never forgive me."

"I've seen news clips of court hearings where people hold up signs. It shows the judge that the public wants the defendant to be held accountable."

"How would we get there?"

"The bus. I looked up the schedule last night. If we leave now, we'd be there in plenty of time." He reached into his backpack and brought out a rolled up tube of paper with a rubber band around it. He unfurled a three-foot-long banner that read KIDS AGAINST ANIMAL CRUELTY. "We can each hold one end," he said. "We'll be powerful pertinent protestors."

I shook my head. "We'd be painfully punished and penalized."

"We could make a difference," Andrew said. "Our presence might be important."

"I can't," I said. "I'm sorry, Andrew, but Mom's doing everything she can to help us rescue Ra. I need to do it her way."

Andrew rolled up his banner and put it away.

When we got back to our room, Mrs. Webster told me she'd talked to my mom and to Heidi Kellogg.

"Class," she said, "we have an opportunity to help another mistreated animal."

Everyone quit talking and paid attention.

"Rusty and Andrew rescued a dog named Ra." Everyone stared at me and Andrew but they were good stares, full of admiration. Andrew grinned at me and I knew he wasn't angry any longer. If we had left school to go to the hearing, we would have missed this.

"Ra got loose yesterday," Mrs. Webster said, "and he is still missing. They need help to find him."

The class immediately buzzed with plans to look for Ra. While they talked, a student helper from the school office came to my classroom with a stack of flyers that said LOST DOG. REWARD. They had Ra's picture and a phone number on them. Mrs. Webster had asked someone at the Humane Society to e-mail the flyer attachment so the school could print them.

Several kids said they'd distribute Lost Dog flyers; some said they'd ride their bikes and look for him; others said they'd e-mail all their relatives.

While Mrs. Webster distributed the flyers, Andrew asked me, "Did you look for Ra at the fort? Maybe he went back there."

I slapped my palm to my forehead. I couldn't believe I had not thought to look around the fort. That had been his safe home, and he was used to being walked there. It made sense that he'd return. What if he'd been sitting at the door of the fort all night?

"I'm the most ignorant person ever born," I told Andrew. "I am a bona fide brainless blob. It never occurred to me that Ra might be there."

"We can look there right after school," Andrew said.

I thought about calling Mrs. Gardiner and asking her to go look at the fort but she uses a cane, and the greenbelt terrain is uneven. What if she fell? I knew Mom wouldn't like it if I called Mrs. Gardiner. Also, the fewer neighbors who knew about the fort, the better. If Ra had gone there, I hoped he would stay and wait for me to come to him.

My row was the last to receive flyers. When Gerald got his, he said, "That's Buddy! That's my uncle's dog! Somebody stole him." Gerald turned in his seat and looked suspiciously at me. "Where'd you get this dog?"

"What's your uncle's name?" I asked.

"Uncle Kip."

"His last name."

"Myers. Kip Myers." Gerald looked back at Mrs. Webster. "His dog was swiped right out of his front yard. The cops didn't do nothing about it, but Uncle Kip says he knows who took Buddy and he's suing them to get Buddy back."

Mrs. Webster looked worried. "Many German shepherds

look alike," she said. "Are you positive this is a picture of your uncle's dog?"

"That's him, all right," Gerald said. "That picture was taken in Uncle Kip's front yard. Now we know for sure who the thieves were!" He gave me a triumphant look, and I knew he was remembering when I caught him stealing dog food out of the donation bin and had called him a thief.

"I agree with Gerald," I said.

"You do?" Gerald said.

"It is the same dog," I said. "We rescued him from the yard of a man who beat him and left him chained up with no food or water. The man's last name is Myers."

I heard murmurs of disbelief from some of my classmates.

"So you admit it!" Gerald said. "You stole my uncle's dog!"

"We rescued him."

Mrs. Webster said, "Quiet, everyone! This situation is more complicated than I realized and won't be an appropriate class project. Please pass the flyers forward."

"I want to keep mine," Hayley said. "I'm going to help find Ra."

"Me too," said Jordan.

"His name isn't Ra," said Gerald. "It's Buddy."

It was clear that the sympathies of the class were with

Andrew and me, not with Gerald, but Mrs. Webster was ada-
mant. "What you do on your own time outside of class is up
to you," she said, "but this will not be a school activity. Please
get out your math workbooks."

I got out my workbook and pretended to look at the problems while my mind mulled over the fact that Mean Man Myers was Gerald's uncle. No wonder Gerald was a jerk if that's
the kind of family he had. I wondered what his parents were
like. Maybe they were as horrible as his uncle, which would
explain a lot about Gerald's behavior.

I wondered why he had tried to steal dog food. Maybe he
had a dog and his parents didn't feed it enough. Maybe he
had planned to give the food to Ra.

I tapped Gerald on the shoulder. He glared at me. "Do
you have a dog?" I whispered.

"Why do you care?"

"Do you have a dog or not?"

"None of your business." He turned back to his math
book.

My temporary sympathy for Gerald evaporated. Probably
he stole the dog food because he couldn't resist a chance to
steal something.

Gerald, I thought, is a rotten repulsive rat.

After school, I rushed to the fort as soon as I got off the
bus. I walked through the trees calling Ra, but he wasn't

there. He wasn't waiting by my house, either. I circled the block once and then went inside to leave my backpack.

Andrew arrived on his bike.

"I need to check the phone messages before we start searching," I said. "Mom put an ID tag on Ra with our phone number on it, so if anyone finds him they'll call us."

There were three messages. We drank lemonade while we listened.

The first message was from Mrs. Gardiner telling us she had not see Ra.

The second was from Heidi Kellogg. "Bad news," she said. "The judge let Mr. Myers off with only a warning."

"We should have gone to court," Andrew said. "Our sign might have helped."

The third message was from Mean Man Myers. "When I get my watchdog back," he said, "I'm coming for revenge."

Andrew and I looked at each other. I left all the messages for Mom to hear.

"We have to find Ra before he does," I said.

I scribbled a note to Mom, in case she got home before we returned: *Andrew and I are riding our bikes to look for Ra.*

We went outside, hopped on our bikes, and began to search.

CHAPTER SIXTEEN

Andrew and I rode around for three hours. We took a staple gun with us and stapled flyers to telephone and electric poles. We saw a mail delivery person and asked him if he'd seen Ra. He hadn't, but he took one of the flyers and said he'd be watchful. He told us he'd once found a stolen bicycle because the kid who owned it had given him a picture of the bike and asked him to look for it on his rounds.

As we worked, I thought how good it was to have a friend to help me, someone I could count on in good times or bad to always take my side. Andrew was there for the fun days of bowling and building a fort and playing with Ra, but he also showed up to distribute flyers and ride for miles, calling and searching. If he had felt unhappy over not seeing the collie's ghost, and for being less involved with Ra than he'd been while Ra lived at the fort, he had put those feelings aside, and I was grateful.

Andrew had to be home by six, so I went home then, too. Mom and I made peanut butter sandwiches for dinner, then ate them in the car while we looked for Ra. I kept my window rolled down despite the cold. I called until my voice was hoarse, shining my flashlight into shrubbery and alleys.

How could he vanish without a trace? Several times we saw one of our Lost Dog flyers and didn't know who had put it up. It helped to know that other people were also searching for Ra.

"He could be anywhere," Mom said as she wearily parked the car back in our garage. "Some kind person might have thought he was a stray and taken him in and is feeding him."

"How could anyone think he's a stray? He has on a collar and a tag. He was dragging the leash behind him."

"Maybe the collar came off. Maybe the leash got caught on a fence or bush and Ra jerked out of the collar. Who knows? All I know is, we can't look any longer tonight."

We trudged inside and checked for messages. There weren't any.

Before we went to bed, Mom and I took flashlights and looked around the fort. Then we walked to the end of our block and back, calling. Finally we gave up and went upstairs for the night.

The collie's ghost woke me. I knew she was there even before I saw her because I felt the icy air next to my bed. She paced back and forth between my bed and the door. For once, I was glad to see her. I had decided this was a good dog ghost who wanted to help Ra. Maybe she knew where he was. Maybe she had found him and would lead me to him. I wished she could tell me her secrets.

I dressed quickly, slid my feet into a pair of flip-flops, and followed her downstairs. I got one of the flashlights that Mom and I had used earlier. I thought about Mean Man Myers and Mom's warning that I shouldn't go walking around alone until this matter was settled. I knew Mom would want me to wake her up, but what would I tell her? That I was following the ghost of a dog?

That day when the ghost dog had tried to block us from getting in the car, Mom had not seen her. She wouldn't be able to see her now, either, so how could I possibly explain why I intended to follow this apparition into the night?

I knew tonight I wouldn't turn back; I would go where the collie's ghost led me. Yet, I also knew that I needed to be careful. I opened Mom's purse, removed her cell phone, and put it in my pocket. I saw a business card for Heidi Kellogg and took that, too. I paused a moment, trying to think what else I might need. My camera? I grabbed it and stuck it in my other pocket.

I wrote a note: *I've gone with the collie. Andrew can explain.* If something awful happened to me and I never came home, at least she'd know why I left.

No! I told myself. Don't be negative. You'll come home. You'll probably return before Mom wakes up and realizes you're gone, and, with any luck, you'll have Ra with you.

I let myself out the front door and trotted down the sidewalk after the collie's ghost. I hoped she had discovered Ra, shut by accident in the garage of someone who was gone for a few days, or maybe she'd found him wandering behind a strip mall, foraging in the Dumpsters for food. Perhaps he was hanging around the parking lot of a fast-food restaurant, begging for handouts. He might be hopelessly lost, running in circles the way people do when they're lost in the woods.

Those possibilities vanished as I realized where the collie's ghost was leading me—straight back to Mean Man Myers's house. Had he found Ra, after all, and somehow managed to force him into the car?

We were still half a block away when I saw Ra lying in the dirt, chained to the tree, exactly where he had been the first time I ever saw him.

I ran to him. He saw me coming and struggled to get up. His tail wagged but I could tell he'd been injured. He staggered briefly, then lay down again. I dropped to my knees and threw my arms around him.

"Oh, Ra!" I whispered. "I'm so glad to see you! I'm taking you home, right now."

I didn't have a leash with me, but I knew I didn't need one. Ra would go with me whether he was leashed or not. Ra's blue collar with the suns on it had been replaced by a choke collar, and when I reached for the chain to unhook it, I discovered that there was a small padlock attached. Ra's collar was locked around his neck and locked to the chain!

As I debated whether to call Heidi Kellogg, knowing I'd probably get voice mail at this hour, or go home and wake up Mom, knowing she'd be angry that I had come here by myself, the ghost dog began nudging me with her nose.

"I found him," I told her. "Thank you. You led me right to him."

The collie nudged again and then trotted toward Mean Man's driveway. She paused and looked back at me, her way of telling me she wanted me to follow her. I shook my head. I'd already found Ra; I had no desire to go closer to the house.

The ghost dog trotted back to me and pushed her head insistently against my thigh. Then she turned and went back to the driveway. Meanwhile, Ra moaned quietly, clearly uncomfortable. I wondered if he had been hit by a car or if Mr. Myers had hurt him again.

I could not imagine why the collie wanted me to walk up that driveway. I had confronted Mr. Myers the day he tried to take Ra, and it hadn't done any good. I sure didn't want to talk to him again.

The only reason I could think of for the ghost to want me to approach that house was if Mr. Myers had another dog in there. Perhaps Ra wasn't the only dog that the ghost wanted me to rescue.

I knew I couldn't do that, not by myself. If another animal needed help, I would go through the proper channels this time rather than plunging in on my own. But I couldn't ask Heidi Kellogg to respond unless I knew for certain that an animal was in danger.

I ran my hand gently down Ra's back. He didn't look able to walk anywhere tonight, even if I could get the padlock off his collar. I'd have to get help and come back for him.

I looked at the ghost dog, who watched me from the edge of the driveway. Her white fur glowed in the moonlight. Somewhere in the distance, a siren screamed, rising and falling urgently, then fading away. I took a deep breath and followed the collie toward Mean Man's house.

The shrubs around the house were denser than I had realized. From the street, they looked like a thick hedge but as the driveway went into that area, I saw that there was more than one row of shrubs, planted close together with their branches intertwined to form a solid barrier. They towered above me, at least ten feet high. One branch snagged my sleeve as I passed, its twiggy fingers hanging on until I pried them loose.

As soon as the driveway passed the hedge, it curved to the right and I saw the house ahead. A white car blocked the driveway near the house; the old blue car was parked in front of it. I walked around them.

As I got closer to the house I smelled a strange odor. I

wrinkled my nose. It stunk like Mom's nail polish. Mr. Myers must have rotting garbage back here. A faint light glowed around the perimeters of three windows, and I realized that all the windows had black panes instead of clear glass. It looked as if they had been painted. I wondered why anyone would do that but at least I didn't have to worry that someone inside would see me approaching.

Trash covered the front porch on both sides of the door. The ghost dog floated a few inches above the clutter, then turned at the door and looked back at me.

I didn't dare turn on my flashlight, but between the small amount of light that seeped from the windows and the almost-full moon, I could see that the litter on the porch wasn't regular garbage. Blue cylinders the size of coffee urns lay on their sides, surrounded by dozens of empty decongestant boxes and bubble packs. A tangle of narrow hoses coiled in one corner like a nest of snakes.

I bent my arm and put my nose in my elbow to dull the odor. That's when it hit me. The smell was ammonia, and the blue cylinders were empty butane containers. The trash on the porch was evidence that Mr. Myers was making methamphetamine in this house! I remembered the man who spoke to our class, the one who told us what to look for if we suspected a meth lab. He had described the smell as being like cat urine or ammonia. He was right.

I shuddered, recalling what else that speaker had told us: people who use meth often become paranoid and delusional as well as irrationally violent. If Mr. Myers was on meth, he was dangerous not only to animals but to anyone he saw.

The ghost dog waited expectantly by the door, but I turned and fled back down the driveway. I hurried along the sidewalk until I was off Mean Man's property. Then I opened Mom's phone and called 911.

I gave my name and reported that I'd found what appeared to be a meth lab. I was connected to a police detective, and this time I knew the address. I told him everything I'd seen. "I'm looking at the house now," I said. "There are people inside."

"Thanks for the good information," the officer said. "We'll look into it."

"Mr. Myers, the man who lives in the house, has my dog locked on a chain in the yard."

"I'll notify Animal Control."

"This isn't a stray dog problem," I said. "Heidi Kellogg in Animal Control is already investigating Mr. Myers for animal cruelty. He took Ra away from me and now Ra's locked on a chain and he's been hurt. He needs to go to the vet."

"What's your phone number?" the officer asked.

I gave him Mom's cell number.

"I'll investigate," he said.

"Please hurry."

Next I called Heidi Kellogg. She had said she sometimes worked late at night, but I got her voice mail. I left a message: "This is Rusty Larson. Mr. Myers has Ra locked on a chain in his yard. Ra's been hurt. I called the police because I think Mr. Myers has a meth lab in his house."

As I closed the phone, I saw that the ghost dog was now lying next to Ra, as if to comfort him.

I knew I should hurry back home, but I was reluctant to leave without Ra. I wished I could call Andrew without waking his parents. His dad might have a tool that would cut through the lock on Ra's collar. I wondered if Mom was still asleep. I didn't want to call and wake her up, but I also didn't want her in a panic, wondering where I was.

A thought teased the edges of my mind like the tide gradually coming in, each wave moving closer than the last. I felt as if I were overlooking something, some action that I ought to take. It was cold out, and I shoved my hands in the pockets of my jacket. As soon as my hand hit the camera, I knew what it was that I should do but hadn't. I needed to take a picture of the items on Mr. Myers's porch.

Although the porch was a mess, it wouldn't take long to put all the trash in bags and haul it off. If that happened, the police could arrive and there'd be no sign of a meth lab except the lingering smell.

The last thing I wanted to do was go back up that drive-way, but I did it anyway. One thing I had learned so far in this whole investigation was that the police needed solid proof, not just accusations.

I walked quickly, noting that there were still lights on behind the blackened windows. When I reached the house, I held the camera up and looked through the viewfinder. I couldn't see much but I aimed it at the porch and hit the but-ton. As the flash went off, the front door opened.

I whirled and ran.

"Who's there?" I recognized Mean Man Myers's voice.

Yard lights came on behind me.

"It's a kid!" said a second man.

"Get him!"

CHAPTER SEVENTEEN

Footsteps thundered behind me.

My shadow ran ahead of me, long and black.

"Stop right there!" yelled Mr. Myers.

I raced on. Until I was past the shrubs, I had no choice but to run straight ahead down the driveway. If I veered to either side, I'd be trapped in Mean Man's yard.

"Stop or I'll shoot!"

Did he really have a gun or was he trying to scare me into stopping? If he had a weapon, I thought, he would use it. Mean Man Myers was the type to shoot first and talk later.

I kept running. My throat felt dry and my temples throbbed. Nervous sweat soaked my T-shirt.

I was almost to the bushes. If I could make it past them, I would turn so that even if Mr. Myers did have a gun, he wouldn't have a straight shot at me. Just a few more yards . . . a few more feet.

I passed the shrubs, but I could tell the men were gaining on me. I should have taken the time to put on my sneakers. Flip-flops were not meant for racing. I cut across the yard toward where Ra lay, heading for the closest neighbor. "Help!" I shouted. "Help me!!"

When I was almost to the tree where Ra was chained, Mr. Myers yelled, "You're done for, boy!" Shocked by how close his voice was, I reached in my pocket for the phone. Before I could open it, his hand clutched the back of my shirt.

I wrenched away from Mean Man's grasp, stumbled, and fell to my knees. As Mr. Myers reached for me, Ra struggled to his feet, launched himself at Mean Man Myers, and sank his teeth into Mean Man's leg. Mean Man sprawled in the dirt, howling. The second man tripped over Ra's chain and went down, too.

Two sets of headlights came down the street. I ran toward them, waving my arms. "HELP!" I shouted.

The cars stopped. Two police officers jumped out and ran toward me.

"They were chasing me," I said, pointing at the men. "They said if I didn't stop, they'd shoot me."

Mr. Myers still lay in the dirt, but the second man was running toward his car. One officer got back in his squad car and drove into the driveway, preventing the man's car from leaving.

The other officer approached Mr. Myers.

"Shoot that dog!" Mr. Myers yelled. "He attacked me. He's vicious!"

"No!" I said. "He's my pet. He only bit because I was

in danger. He was protecting me. He saved my life!"

"Get in the backseat of my car," the officer told me, "and stay there."

I did, but I left the door open so I could hear.

Ra had let go of Mean Man's leg and was lying down again, his head on his paws.

"The kid was trespassing," Mr. Myers said. "He was sneaking around my place taking pictures." He groaned and grabbed his leg. "You need to take him in, lock him up in juvie."

The officer examined Mr. Myers's leg. Soon an ambulance arrived and Mr. Myers was loaded into it. Meanwhile, the second squad car drove out of the driveway with the man who had chased me in the backseat.

As I watched all of this, I began to tremble. The relief I felt was so enormous that I couldn't stop. I sat there, shaking as hard as Ra had the day we almost gave him back to Mean Man Myers.

When the ambulance left, the officer who had examined Mean Man returned to the squad car. "Are you Rusty Larson?" he asked.

I nodded. "I didn't think you'd come so soon. I thought you would have to get a search warrant."

"Before we can get a search warrant, we need evidence that one is justified. When I checked police records, I learned that this house is occupied by a convicted felon, and I got concerned about you being here with your dog. That's why two of us responded."

"Ra is my dog," I said. "Mr. Myers has him locked on that chain so I can't take him home."

The officer said, "I'll have to notify animal control about the dog. He did bite a person."

"Heidi Kellogg from animal control knows all about Ra," I said. "She's been pursuing cruelty charges against Mr. Myers but the judge only gave him a warning. She knows Ra's had all his shots and that he's a friendly dog."

I started to cry. I couldn't help it. "Please," I said. "Please get Ra unlocked and let me take him home. I think he's hurt bad; he should go to a vet."

"I need to talk to your parents," the officer said.

Sooner or later I was going to have to tell Mom what had happened. I might as well get it over with.

I took out Mom's phone and called home. I could tell by the way Mom said, "Hello?" that she had been asleep, which was probably a good thing. By hearing my voice, she knew I was okay before she realized I wasn't home.

"Hi, Mom," I said.

"Rusty! Where are you?"

"I'm at Mr. Myers's house and—"

"What? What are you doing there? Are you okay?" She no longer sounded sleepy.

"It's a long story but I'll have to explain later. Right now, a police officer wants to talk to you."

CHAPTER EIGHTEEN

While we waited for Mom to arrive, the officer made a call. Then he told me, "The other officer saw evidence of a meth lab when he followed the second suspect to his car. That suspect's being booked now. We'll get a search warrant and go inside the house."

When Mom got there, she told the detective everything that had happened with Ra. He used a bolt cutter to get the padlock off Ra's collar. He carefully removed the choke collar and the chain and helped us lift Ra into our car. Ra whimpered when we moved him but he didn't struggle. I think he knew we were trying to help him.

Mom and I took Ra to a twenty-four-hour emergency veterinary clinic where he was examined and had another X-ray. The vet told us it looked as if Ra had recently been hit by a car. I wondered if Mean Man had found Ra on the side of the road or if his own car had done the damage.

Ra's rear leg was broken—the same leg that had been broken once before and never set. He had other injuries, too, including two cracked ribs. "I'm amazed that he could defend you," the vet told me. "It would cause him great pain to move that way. He must love you very much."

I fought back tears. "I love him, too," I said.

Mom turned pale when she learned what it would cost to treat Ra's injuries, but she agreed to do it, including twenty-five extra dollars for a shot of painkiller.

"Please give him that right away," she said.

Surgery on Ra's leg was scheduled for the next morning.

As we drove home, Mom said, "What on earth were you thinking, Rusty? Whatever possessed you to go over there alone in the middle of the night?"

"If I tell you, you won't believe me."

"Try me," she said.

"I followed a ghost," I said. "A dog ghost."

"Oh, Rusty. This is no time for foolish stories. You're already in big trouble, young man, and you'll only make it worse if you don't tell me the truth."

"See?" I said. "I knew you wouldn't believe me."

There were a few seconds of silence. Then Mom said, "A dog ghost?"

"It's the ghost of a collie," I said. "She looks like an ordinary collie except she's all white and I can see through her."

She gave me a sideways glance. "You're serious, aren't you?"

"Yes." I told her everything—how the ghost dog came to my room, how she seemed to be trying to help Ra. I told her how the collie had tried to prevent us from driving Ra to Mean Man's house that day, and how I had taken two photos of the ghost.

"Did Andrew see this ghost?" Mom asked.

"No, but Ra can see it. They sniff noses."

Mom sighed. "I'm glad you didn't say anything about this to the police," she said. "The tabloid papers would never leave us alone."

"It seemed better to say I had been out looking for Ra."

It was after three when I finally laid my head on my pillow and closed my eyes. I wanted to skip school and sleep in the next morning, but Mom wouldn't let me.

"Studies show that sleep deprived children do poorly in school," I said.

"Other studies show that kids who sneak out at night should lose their computer privileges."

While we ate breakfast, Mom listened to the morning news on the radio. One story reported the arrest of Kip Myers and Gerald Langston for possession and manufacture of methamphetamine. My jaw dropped. *Gerald Langston? Was the second drug dealer the father of my classmate?* Both men, according to the report, had prior convictions for assault and for burglary.

Then the reporter said, "A student at Heath Middle

School, Rusty Larson, recognized the signs of a meth lab after learning about them in class. He tipped off the police."

I was so shocked to hear my name on the radio that I dropped my spoon into my bowl of cereal, splashing milk all over.

While I was mopping up the table, Heidi Kellogg called. Mom told her about Ra's condition, then handed me the phone.

"Congratulations, Rusty," Heidi said. "Not only did you discover an illegal drug lab, but you gave me the evidence I needed to refile the cruelty charges."

"But we can't prove that it was Mr. Myers who hurt Ra," I said.

"No, but he didn't seek help for Ra's injuries. Not only that, there was another dog inside the house. A Rottweiler this time. He was half starved, the same as Ra and the Labrador puppy, and his filthy crate was too small. Apparently, Mr. Myers mistreated the dogs and didn't feed them enough because he wanted them to be mean so they'd prevent anyone from coming on his property and discovering what he was doing there."

"What a scumbag," I said. Then I started to laugh. "He wanted Ra to be mean but he's the only one who got bit. Twice!"

"I'll win the case this time," Heidi said. "Of course, Mr. Myers will be in prison anyway."

Mom pointed to her watch and I knew I had to leave for school. Her one concession to my late night had been to say she'd drive me, which meant I could leave ten minutes later than when I rode the school bus.

I had called Andrew as soon as I got up and told him the whole story. He greeted me when I walked into Mrs. Webster's room. "Hail the helpful hero!" he cried, and extended his hand for a high five.

Other kids crowded around. Some had heard the radio broadcast that morning. The news had spread quickly through the halls of Heath.

"I heard your name on the news," Jordan said.

"You're a celebrity!" said Lexi.

"Are you going to be on *Oprah*?" asked Hayley.

Mrs. Webster beamed. "I knew my guest speakers were worthwhile," she said, "but I didn't expect such dramatic results."

I looked at my classmates' excited faces. All but one. Gerald Langston sat as still as a stone, staring at his desk. Matthew walked over and stood beside Gerald. I expected Matthew to ask, "Have you seen the jailbird lately?" and I would not have blamed him one bit for saying it. Instead, he patted Gerald's shoulder, and then walked to his own desk without speaking.

I decided not to say anything more in class about what had

happened with Mr. Myers and Gerald's dad the night before. Instead I said, "The best part of all this is that I got Ra back and he's going to be okay. He's having surgery today but he gets to come home late this afternoon. Andrew and I will be taking care of him. We rescued him together, and we'll both help him heal."

Some of the kids who had been congratulating me turned to thump Andrew on the back. He grinned at me.

At lunch, Andrew asked, "Will the Humane Society release Ra for adoption now that Mr. Myers is in jail?"

"I don't know. I was in a rush this morning when I talked to Ms. Kellogg, and I didn't ask."

It turned out that I didn't have to ask because Mom did it for me. After we picked up Ra that afternoon, she said, "Because Ra was a Humane Society dog when this happened, they are paying his vet bills. People donate to a special fund that's used in cases like this, when an animal needs surgery or extra veterinary care."

"But you were willing to pay it," I said. "Last night when you gave permission, you didn't know the Humane Society would take care of the bill."

"That's true," she said. "After what Ra did for you, we had to help him no matter what it cost."

I was almost afraid to ask the next question. "Does that mean we can adopt him?"

"We already did," Mom said. "I went to the Humane Society this morning after I dropped you at school. Mr. Myers signed papers last night relinquishing all claims to Ra, the Lab puppy, and the Rottweiler."

"He did? After the fuss he made over wanting to keep Ra, I never expected him to do that."

"He probably thought he'd get off easier on the drug charge if he cooperated about the dogs," Mom said. "Since this meant Ra was officially available for adoption, I signed the adoption papers and paid the fee. I also called the emergency clinic right away, and while Ra was anesthetized for his leg surgery, he got neutered and microchipped. Ra's part of our family now."

Ra stuck his nose into the front seat and nudged my arm. I patted his head.

"Good dog," I said. Then I looked at Mom and added, "Good Mom."

I heard the phone ringing as we took Ra into the house.

"Have you read tonight's paper?" Andrew asked.

"Not yet."

"Go get it. I'll wait."

I returned to the phone.

"Page three," Andrew said.

I turned to page three. LOCAL METH LAB BUSTED.

"Got it."

"Read the third paragraph."

I read: *Mr. Langston insisted at first that he had nothing to do with the meth lab. He swore he had never set foot on the property before and was there only to look at a refrigerator that Mr. Myers had advertised for sale. However, the police had a dated photo, from a related investigation into animal cruelty, of Mr. Langston's car parked in Mr. Myers's driveway a week ago. When he saw it, he admitted that he and Myers are brothers-in-law.*

"Wow!" I said. "That was my photo!"

"I thought so. Way to go, Mighty Muscles Man!"

"The first time I followed the collie's ghost there in the night, I took a picture of two cars in the driveway, and I sent it to Heidi Kellogg. I never dreamed it would be proof that Mr. Langston had been there before."

"Speaking of pictures," Andrew said, "Wendy printed out the two that you e-mailed to me and, guess what? I can see the ghost!"

I was so surprised I couldn't respond.

"Wendy handed them to me without saying anything, so I didn't know what they were, and when I looked, there was the collie in front of your bedroom door. She looked exactly the way you had described her. I can see her in the other picture, too, standing beside Ra in Mr. Myers's yard."

"That's great," I said. "I'm really glad."

"You want to hear the strange part? Wendy and I showed the pictures to our parents and they don't see her."

When I showed the photos to Mom the next day, she didn't see the collie's ghost, either. Andrew and I agreed not to show the pictures to anyone else.

I never saw the collie's ghost again. I suspect she wanted me to go up that driveway so I would discover the Rottweiler and rescue it. The rescue didn't happen the way she thought it would, but it did happen. Because of all the publicity about the case, both the black Lab puppy and the Rottweiler were quickly adopted.

Due to the overwhelming evidence, Mr. Myers and Gerald Langston, Sr., pleaded guilty to the drug charges. Since they both had prior convictions, they got long prison sentences. Heidi Kellogg also won a cruelty conviction against Mr. Myers, and the judge ruled that he could not own any more animals.

Gerald, Jr., quit attending Heath Middle School two days after his dad was arrested. We heard that he had gone to live with his grandparents in another state.

That Friday, Andrew said he couldn't come to visit Ra after school. "Mom and Dad are taking Wendy to the Humane Society to deliver her cat blankets," he said, "and I want to ride along."

He called while I was eating dinner. "You have to come over here," he said. "Right away!"

"What's up?"

"You'll see. Ask your mom to drive you."

Mom agreed.

When Andrew opened the door, a beautiful German shepherd stood beside him, wagging her tail.

"Meet Cleopatra," Andrew said.

"Cleo, for short," said Wendy.

I let the dog sniff my hand.

"While Wendy was giving her cat blankets to the Humane Society staff," Andrew said, "I looked to see if the dog we'd seen on our field trip was still there. She was."

"We begged Mom and Dad to let us have her," Wendy said.

"I said I'd take good care of her, just like we did with Ra," Andrew said.

"I told them if they let us take her, I'd never whine again," Wendy added.

I figured that probably cinched the deal.

"She was already spayed," Andrew said, "so we got to bring her home with us right away."

"She's beautiful," I said. "Bring her over tomorrow so she and Ra can play together."

• • •

Both dogs seemed glad to have a dog friend. They chased each other, played tug-of-war with a rope toy, and then stretched out together for a nap while Andrew and I did our homework.

The next time Andrew and I decided to go bowling, I asked Wendy if she wanted to go with us.

"Nope," she said. "I'm busy. I've started my own club, the Kitty Knitters. There are three other members. Grandma taught them how to knit and we meet every Saturday to make blankets for the shelter cats."

"You're a fine friend to felines," I said.

"Before I do any more cat blankets, I'm knitting special blankets for Ra and Cleo." She held up a knitted piece the size of the kitchen stove, made from garish purple and chartreuse yarn. "This one's for Ra," she said. It was the ugliest thing I'd ever seen.

"He'll love it," I told her. "Thanks, Wendy."

Mom drove us to the bowling alley. Partway there we passed a yard where a dog was tied to the fence.

"Mom, look!" I cried. "That dog was left tied up alone!"

"Not again!" she said. She pulled over, then backed up to get a better look. "He has a bowl of water and a snug doghouse," she said.

"The yard is clean," Andrew said. "He's wearing a collar and a dog tag."

"I guess he's okay then," I said. "We won't need to rescue him."

"Thank goodness," Mom said as she headed for the bowling alley.

PURR—FECT CAT BLANKETS

Materials

- 100% acrylic yarn
- Size 15 knitting needles

Using two strands of 4-ply yarn, cast on 33 stitches.
Knit every row for 66 rows—there will be 33 ridges.
Cast off.

The blanket will measure approximately 15 x 12 inches.
Blankets can be made all one color or by joining leftovers from other projects. The cats do not care how they look.
Two 6-ounce skeins will make two blankets with leftovers.

THANK YOU TO:

Detective Robert Onishi of the Renton, Washington, Police Department for patiently answering all my questions about police procedure.

The Pierce County, Washington, Sheriff's Department for information about meth labs.

Pasado's Safe Haven for information about cruelty investigations.

Diana Sigalla for cat blanket knitting instructions.

The Buckley, Washington, Public Library for a never-ending source of research material.

Animal cruelty is against the law in every state in the United States. Learn how to help:
www.aspca.org/fight-animal-cruelty/top-10-ways-to-prevent-animal.html.

Learn more about puppy mills:
www.hsus.org

Learn more about ghosts at:
www.ghostresearch.org